HER OWN
ROBINSON CRUSOE

Serena Winter normally reports on local events for a travel magazine. Now she's landed her dream job in the Caribbean. On the Atlantic crossing, she's seated next to a grumpy stranger: 'Broderick Loveday, doing nothing and going nowhere,' he tells her. Her job is to report back to 'The Explorer' magazine on drunken monkeys and anything interesting in the islands. The kindness of locals — and someone special — keeps her heart in the Caribbean. But what about when the time comes to leave?

SUSAN JONES

HER OWN ROBINSON CRUSOE

Complete and Unabridged

LINFORD
Leicester

First published in Great Britain in 2018

First Linford Edition
published 2020

A catalogue record for this book is available
from the British Library.

ISBN 978–1–4444–4627–0

Published by
Ulverscroft Limited
Anstey, Leicestershire

Set by Words & Graphics Ltd.
Anstey, Leicestershire
Printed and bound in Great Britain by
TJ Books Limited, Padstow, Cornwall

This book is printed on acid-free paper

1

'Christmas in the Caribbean, what more could a girl want?' Only a few days ago, Serena Winter had spoken to her mum on the phone . . . 'I'm the only travelling reporter for Explorer magazine who hasn't come down with the awful flu bug — otherwise they'd never have sent me.

'Imagine! My first proper assignment, Mum. I'd be daft not to take it — only thing is, it means being away for Christmas. You're sure you don't mind me not joining you and Dad this year?'

She heard the reassurance in her mother's voice, and then continued.

'All I have to do is send back some stories about the drunken monkeys that are supposed to inhabit some of the Caribbean islands, and any other interesting topics I think readers might like. Shouldn't be too difficult, should it?'

She packed a haversack with her laptop, pens, notebooks, combat trousers and T-shirts. She booked a rare appointment at the hairdresser and had braids put in her long, blonde hair to keep it tidy and save on shampoo. Sun block, bikinis and a sarong were added to her bag.

The company had reserved a bungalow for the duration of her stay on the Caribbean island of Neptune. She would hire a boat and visit as many of the islands as possible during her stay.

★   ★   ★

The man next to her on the plane, who sat in the window seat, had a shaggy mop of dark hair, greying at the temples, and a substantial beard. Not that she was taking any notice, of course — only his dark grey eyes looked somehow familiar. They reminded her of someone.

2

He glanced up from his in-flight magazine when the flight attendant rattled along with the trolley.

'My usual vodka and orange, thanks.'

The woman handed him the drink, which looked, Serena thought, a generous measure. There was no mistaking the twinkle in her eye.

That was the first time Serena had heard him speak, and from the way the flight attendant was fawning, she obviously knew him. Why she was making so much fuss over such a tramp-like guy was mystifying. Then again, wasn't it all part of the crew's job to make everyone feel welcome?

Serena helped herself to a sparkling water with slice of lemon. 'Thank you.' She smiled at the flight attendant. Settling back in her seat, she sneaked a glance at the stranger sipping his iced vodka and orange.

She decided to ask, 'Are you going on holiday, or . . . ?' From the way he was dressed, quite casually to say the least, she imagined him to be some kind of

3

outdated bush ranger. 'I'm Serena Winter, reporter for Explorer magazine.'

There was a phrase she'd never tire of saying.

His grey eyes turned on her, hard as granite.

'Nature, local colour — not celebrity gossip or anything like that,' she explained hastily.

'That's nice for you. I'm Broderick Loveday, doing nothing, going nowhere, for no man's magazine.' His look made it clear he wasn't interested in anything she had to say.

The name sounded familiar . . . No, that was some article she read a while back, about a Lord Loveday. Had he been involved in a stock market scandal?

Another glance and she decided he couldn't be related to that man. The one in the article had been lush, dressed to kill with eyes to fall into. Other than his mysterious eyes, ethereal almost, there was no hint of this

4

misery-guts being anything interesting.

For the rest of the journey, Serena flipped between ghost stories and romance on her tablet. Not everyone was as chatty as she was, and maybe the scruff by her side wasn't happy in his home life. Either way, she left him to his magazine and vodka.

She watched the hazy mountains in the distance coming closer and the clear waters of the Caribbean sparkling like a myriad tiny diamonds as the plane descended, ready for landing at the Joseph Rolando airport. A bubble of excitement fizzed through her as the plane gently bumped down on the Tarmac and cruised along the runway. The jolt was only slight. She could hardly wait to get off the plane and settle into what would be her home for the next month.

The company she worked for had allocated some extra time as she was owed a few holiday days, and the magazine offices were to be closed all over Christmas and New Year. Serena planned to make the most of it.

'Now to find those drunken monkeys!' she announced cheerfully.

Broderick had been napping. His hair stuck up and his beard curled under his chin as if he'd never shaved in his life. Serena smiled as she remembered the flight attendant retrieving his tipped-up glass from his hand before they prepared to land.

Not sure whether he'd heard a word, she watched him waking and wondered whether she may have found herself a real live drunken monkey without even stepping off the plane.

His eyes opened. He looked reserved for a second, then glanced out of his window.

'What were you saying?' He stifled a yawn.

'Drunken monkeys, have you ever seen them?'

Serena felt a giggle building up at the thought of a monkey guzzling on a cocktail or gin and tonic, and couldn't help wondering if they nicked a packet of crisps at the same time, to go with it.

'That'll be St Kitts — only don't say I didn't warn you.'

She grabbed her belongings and joined the queue headed towards the exit door, then turned.

'Warn me? You didn't even speak to me.'

Making her way slowly up the aisle, Serena decided she didn't want to waste an opportunity. She was the roving reporter, and he might have something worth writing home about. Turning back to where he was just leaving his seat, she called, 'Let me buy you coffee.' She pointed towards the airport. 'Then you can tell me what it was you were warning me about.'

He looked away without responding and the reporter in her was piqued; he looked the type who could lead her to places she'd never find on her own. Pity he'd been so distracted and distant.

Serena stepped out into the sunshine.

7

Already she heard reggae music drifting on the breeze. She needed a cool drink, and then a taxi to her destination. The slip of paper with directions to the bungalow was safe in her haversack.

She turned her face to the sky and savoured the moment. *This is the job of a lifetime, Serena Winter, and you need to enjoy every moment, starting right now.* The scent of blossom and oranges made her feel instantly happier.

The Rocky Creek café in the airport lounge was open and Serena wondered if the coffee would be the special Blue Mountain type she liked to buy from the supermarket back home. As she fiddled with her purse and attempted to find the correct dollars, a deep voice behind her sounded familiar.

'Never mind that, I've got Caribbean dollars, save your cash for another day.' Before she had chance to reply, the man in the khaki cut-offs and the crumpled shirt to match was ordering coffee for two and a maple syrup bar to go with it. He gathered the tray and placed it on a nearby table.

'Look, I was king of the grumps for most of the flight.' He shoved his wallet into the back pocket of his shorts and held his hands up in submission. 'Let me make up for it. You'll soon taste the best coffee you'll ever drink around here.' He pushed a firm hand through his unruly hair. 'It's worth coming home for, and now I'm back on Caribbean soil, things are brighter already.'

He smiled and his eyes crinkled at the corners. All of a sudden he looked a lot less desolate.

'Looks and smells divine, but I really fancy a cool drink. Not trying to be awkward, Broderick, only with the heat and . . . '

Before she could finish, he was back at the counter laughing and joking with the proprietor. She heard him saying something about him getting hot and the lady wanted cold. He turned to ask, 'They've got Sprite, orange, what would you like?'

She settled on tonic water with a slice of lime.

Being alone never bothered Serena; it was normal for her. But on arrival, to have some company from the man who had been beside her for most of the day wasn't unwelcome. Maybe he would give her exclusive information on the island — and the surrounding ones, even. Then it would be easy to get rid of him once they'd had a chat and finished the drinks.

He did seem to know quite a few people here. She wasn't sure if she'd missed some of what he was saying as he returned to the table.

'I could have made a bit more effort to chat during the flight, only I really felt whacked out. Trips never agree with me. Turned out the whole thing was a waste of time anyway.'

He looked genuinely sorry. Serena didn't think he'd even done anything to be sorry for, other than being a bit rude. He was a total stranger, and as a rule she wouldn't be sitting in an airport café drinking coffee and chatting about travel with someone she'd only just met.

For the sake of the job, though, she believed it necessary — and there was something endearing about him. He was rustic in a Robinson Crusoe-type way.

'I'm on an assignment.' She plumped for the business-like approach, to let him know she wasn't some silly kid.

'Drunken monkeys, you said.' He sipped his coffee, relaxing visibly. 'They'll watch for you turning your back or going for a swim in the pool and then swipe the drink. They're the bad boys of the islands. We should get a rehab sanctuary going. There are places to find them only a boat ride from here. You'll have to see a chap called Nicky. He takes his yacht around the islands all day long; he'll be the one to put you right. Tell him Brodders sent you.'

Serena pushed her braided hair behind her shoulder and rested her chin on her hand while she studied the

11

rough-looking man who'd ignored her for hours and now bought her the most delicious coffee she'd ever tasted.

'You're some kind of a ranger, then? I guessed that from the way you're dressed.'

He threw his head back and laughed loudly for the first time since she'd been in his company — a real belly laugh. Then he wiped his eyes and sat up. Back was the serious face and solemn gaze.

'You guessed wrong. I'm not any kind of ranger, other than a lone one, and what better place to get lost in?' He threw his arms out wide and made big eyes and a crazy face.

Serena knew it was time to depart. Yet she almost looked upon Broderick as a friend now, and part of her worried that he'd be alone. Something in the way he was so quick to dismiss company made him seem more vulnerable than the independent chap he made himself out to be.

'Is anyone coming to pick you up?'

she asked, trying not to show how concerned she was. He couldn't be as alone as he made out, surely?

'I rather hoped the flight attendant might pick me up, but no such luck.' He glanced over to where a couple of uniformed ladies were laughing and chatting to other cabin crew. 'That was a joke, by the way. I'm happy the way I am. Good luck with the articles, then.' He stood abruptly and gave her a curt nod and was gone as quickly as he'd come.

Serena searched for the scrap of paper that told her she needed to find Ackee Grove Cottage, somewhere along the coast. Sending a quick email simply stating *The Eagle has landed!* she gathered her things and made her way to the taxi rank — too late. A couple had just jumped into the last available cab, which sped off before she had chance to raise her hand.

She stood back, imagining that another one would be along soon. The screech of brakes made her turn. An open-topped Jeep with Broderick at the wheel pulled up alongside.

'Well, seeing as the last cab just went, there's no point you waiting and paying for a taxi when this is available. Jump in.' He turned to check nothing was behind, waiting to pass. As she hesitated, he continued, 'You can wait around and see if another one comes, or I'll drop you to where you're going, by the quickest route. Your choice, I can't wait around all day.'

He tapped his fingers on the wheel and stared straight ahead, waiting for her to decide.

Serena looked up and down the road, and reasoned she'd rather share a lift with someone she'd already met for her journey to Ackee Grove, even if it was Mr Madness himself with the crazy hair and thick black beard.

In all fairness, he couldn't be half as crazy as he made out — otherwise folk wouldn't have made such a fuss of him during the last half hour in the café, and on the plane.

For all his eccentric ways and his earthy looks, he wasn't short of admiring looks from the ladies, she'd noted. Men appeared to respect him as well, so she felt in no danger getting into his Jeep. Gathering her bags, she jumped in beside him and held on tight as he sped off rather more quickly than she'd anticipated.

She'd sat next to him for more than ten hours on the flight from London, yet he'd been so quietly engrossed in his magazine or sleeping that she'd hardly had chance to get to know him at all — other than surmising that he was glad to be leaving behind whatever it was he'd left. He still hadn't said what, or who, it was — and, Serena reminded herself, she was too preoccupied with her task in hand and getting to her lodgings to worry about Broderick Loveday's backstory. Maybe if she got to know him better he'd tell her?

She smoothed out her now crinkled piece of paper showing details of where she would find her lodgings.

'You haven't asked how far you'll need to drive.' She gave him a sidelong glance. 'I'm headed for a place called Fishstone Bay.'

Broderick gave a quiet snigger.

'You and all the other latest incomers. Oh, and did they tell you that once you've visited Neptune you either stay here, or . . . '

Something made him stop speaking.

'Stay here or what? Don't tell me half a story and then go quiet.' Serena was in no mood for any more long silences.

He shook his hair until it resembled a mop. She wanted to laugh but knew it wasn't appropriate, sensing the mood he was plunging into. Then he spoke.

'Let's just say, because I have a feeling you'll keep asking if I don't tell you. After a while, if you try to go back, there's no point. And don't ask any more questions, otherwise you can find a taxi. Now then, what part of Fishstone Bay do you want?'

'A place called Ackee Grove. We can

16

ask someone when we get there, maybe.'

Broderick was focusing on the road and she wondered if he'd forgotten he had a passenger.

He had a warm, deep voice. She felt more at ease when he was chatting so she slipped into her normal ways of talking rather too much, to get him to respond.

'Do you live nearby? I'd hate for you to be going too far out of your way. It's really kind of you to give me a lift as well.'

'I'm an islander — not from this one, another one. Not the drunken monkey one, before you say it.' He gave her a half-smile. 'They will drive you crazy if you don't watch out.' He threw a glance at her camera slung around her neck. 'They'll soon twig on and leave you alone if you stick to non-alcoholic drinks. At least you'll have some peace in the lodgings. As far as I know, they haven't made their way to Neptune yet.'

He drove along winding lanes and

17

then over a crossroads. Serena took in the lush palms in the distance and banana trees in what looked like a farmland area. A mist rolled over the tops of distant trees and the tang of salt air was a tonic. She felt amazingly relaxed, considering the daredevil tactics of her driver.

Unwrapping cookies she'd saved from the flight, Serena took one bite, then pulled a face.

'Yuck — hardly edible, and not nearly as good as those bars you bought in the café.'

'Wait until you try the food here. You won't want biscuits. The wild fruits and yams . . . mmm, you'll find out. Until you've eaten freshly caught lobster cooked over a camp fire, you haven't lived.'

He turned and smiled. Gone was Mr Grumps; a man with a twinkle in his eye and a warm nature began to shine through. Being with him gave her a warm feeling now.

Serena shook her braids and turned

her face to the warmth of the sun. 'What about the time difference? I was thinking it's about mid-afternoon, but is it?'

'Look at the sun.' He pointed. 'We're five hours behind the UK here, and with a ten-hour flight, you do the maths.'

Serena used her fingers to work out that if she'd left on an early flight at seven o'clock, it would be five o'clock, UK time. That made it around midday now, roughly speaking, and from looking at the sun, she should have guessed that.

'Of course I knew that — only testing.' She chewed on her lower lip and gave a mocking scowl. 'Clever clogs. So what do you do for a living, Mr Broderick Loveday? And you haven't told me the name of the island you live on.'

With the heat and excitement of being in a land far away from her mundane office job in St Ives, Serena was feeling increasingly confident.

'If you look out over there . . . ' He swung into a passing place and drew the Jeep to a halt. The abrupt stop sent brown dust flying up from under the front wheel, causing Serena to cough.

Before he had chance to point out any landmarks, Serena had jumped out and leaned over the wall. A breeze ruffled her skirt, and she put her hand down to stop it blowing up.

'Wow! It's like something out of a travel brochure.' Never in her dreams had she seen so much blue and felt so alive. Turning to her driver, she clasped her hands. Words simply couldn't describe how she felt.

★ ★ ★

Back on the road again, it became evident that the rambling trip to her destination would have been near-impossible without Brockerick and his Jeep. Serena almost fell into him when they lunged down yet another pot hole, but the surroundings and smiling faces of locals waving as they passed more than made up for the road surface. An old sign with *Ackee* showing and the rest worn off swung in the afternoon breeze.

'Looks like this might be it.' He yanked the handbrake on and switched the engine off.

A small shack with a red roof stood between thickets of greenery and gigantic flowering shrubs.

Serena was put in mind of a quaint cottage like the ones her family had stayed in on holidays in Devon when she was small. The front was out of sight, she realised. It was the back of the dwelling they had come across first of all.

She reached for her bags and looked at Broderick, wondering whether he'd drive off, or wait and have a look around the lodgings.

'Would you like to stay for tea?' she asked.

She wanted him to hang around for a while; there might be something he would be able to help her with. And she didn't want to see him drive off just yet.

The pale blue stucco walls looked rather quirky, she thought, and rambling exotic flowers trailed peachy trumpets, adding to the sugar-plum cotton candy air of the house.

'That's an allamanda. Lovely to look at, but deadly to hold. Don't touch it, whatever you do . . . Only letting you know what's what.' Broderick gave her what looked like a hint of a wink. 'You might write an article on it.'

Now she knew he was making fun.

'Are you going to have a quick look round before you dash off?'

He was beginning to irritate her a little, and she wondered at his laid-back attitude about getting back to his own island.

Serena followed the crazy paving round to the front of the small abode, only to find a wooden door rather resembling a stable entrance, with the top half hanging open.

'The key will be under the nearest rock to the door. It's a rule of the locals.' Broderick strolled up to the swinging top half of door and leaned in and unlatched the bottom part. 'Only you won't need the key, it's open already.' He turned and grinned. 'This is more like Starfish Bay than Fishstone Bay. Sure you've got the right place?' Another rusty old sign swinging in the warm evening breeze confirmed it to be *Ackee* something. The last part had worn away.

Serena stepped inside with a touch of trepidation. She found a box of matches on a worktop, and a torch. The electric lights didn't seem to be working.

'How odd — they said it was well-equipped. This is more of a shanty shack.'

The smell of damp was unmistakable, and she could swear she saw a creature resembling a rat darting into a hole in the skirting board.

'Aarrgh! This place is infested. I daren't look in the bedroom. There's probably a drunken monkey in the bed.' She clung to Broderick, holding his hand tightly without realising.

'It just needs airing, that's all. These shacks soon go damp if left unattended.'

He pushed open a rattan door, leading to where a bed with a modest mattress awaited. A pile of brightly coloured throws and bedding lay on a trunk at the side of the bed.

'Are they serious?' Serena looked around at the bedroom and the huge mosquito net which hung over the headboard.

'You'll need that — and I hope you've got spray or cream to keep those mossies away.'

He had a half-smile playing around his lips, which didn't go unnoticed by Serena.

'You think this is funny?' She threw her bags onto the floor and slumped in a heap on the bed.

'Not that — only how it's gone from the trip of a lifetime to a holiday from hell, by the look on your face. It's only because you're tired, and probably hungry. How about I fetch a couple of curries from the place back there?' He indicated the route they'd come in on. 'Then we can have a last supper together before I go on my way.'

Serena could only nod. That sounded ideal, apart from the bit about him going on his way. In a short space of time, she'd grown surprisingly fond of her eccentric island man. There was something about his quiet ways. He made her feel comfortable, safe and secure.

Still, she had a job to do. Tomorrow she would hire a boat and go in search of drunken monkeys.

* * *

'There's a hotel only half a mile further up the road.' Broderick had returned with vegetarian curry and rice for two. It was all Serena could do to stop herself from giving him a hug when she heard him saying he'd booked her into there.

She ate hungrily; the curry was delicious with a fruity taste that she wasn't familiar with.

'But this is my place. The company are paying. Maybe I could try and get used to it . . . '

She doubted it, and now she felt guilty for moaning and making him feel obliged to help out when he really wanted to get home.

'I'm not paying — well, only for a couple of days. By then you'll have had time to get in touch with your magazine cronies and tell them what's happened. Or you can get this place cleared out. It'll be great once it's aired a bit.' He finished his curry and stood up. 'Come on, I'll drop you off at The Atlantis, and then be on my way. Welcome to the Caribbean — you'll come to love it as much as I do by time you've been here a while.'

He gathered her bags and headed to the Jeep.

The Atlantis had a reception, twenty rooms, a heated outdoor pool and a gym. Now Serena was back in her comfort zone. What were they thinking, renting out a damp shed for her to stay in? As soon as she was settled in, she'd be sending a heated email. If it weren't for Robinson Crusoe, she'd be stuck in a rat-infested hovel.

As she waved him off from her balcony, she wondered whether she'd see him again. They'd made no arrangements. He was probably glad to be rid of her after paying out for curry and lodgings — though she'd offered repeatedly and he'd refused to take a penny. She had a feeling there was more to him than he was showing.

As she drifted off to sleep on silky-soft sheets in an air-conditioned room, with refreshments laid out on her bedside table, drunken monkeys were the last thing on her mind.

2

The sound of crickets had kept Serena awake for most of the night. 'Listen out for the gleep-gleep sound of tree frogs,' a couple of other guests had told her earlier.

She'd been tired, but sleep just wouldn't come. Maybe it was the sheer excitement of landing in the Caribbean, or meeting one of the strangest men she'd ever encountered that kept her awake. The shock from finding the shack, which was supposed to have been home, played on her mind as well. There was no doubt she'd have been eaten alive by some creature if she'd stayed there.

Quickly showering and getting changed into light combats and blouse, she pulled open her laptop and dashed off a none-too friendly email.

I didn't stay at the broken down

shack. Even though it had lovely plants covering the walls — deadly to the touch, I'm told. It was the sight of the giant rat that decided it, just to let you to know. A kind stranger booked me into the Hotel Atlantis with sea view, heated pool and Wi-Fi. Will get to work immediately, and Robinson Crusoe will invoice Explorer magazine for two nights in this place. Regards, Serena W.

Not sure where I'll be staying after that, but will find somewhere more habitable.

Hitting the Send button hard gave her some minor satisfaction, but when an email came pinging straight back, she sat on the edge of her bed and studied the screen.

Ackee Grove Cottage, modernised kitchen, en-suite bedroom, outdoor pool maintained by a caretaker who will meet you on arrival. Click on the link and this is where you're supposed to be.

Did you take a detour? You should have contacted us yesterday. Some *mistake has occurred, and who is Robinson Crusoe?*

Regards,

Rita Parker

Features Editor for Explorer magazine.

Serena clicked on the link. Ackee Grove Cottage had a terrace adorned with table and chairs with a little wooden rail around the edge, painted white, like in the Western films she watched as a girl. The place looked fabulous, and welcoming. Rather like something from *Pollyanna*. There was even a picture of the local man, Pedro, who would be the cleaner/cook and general handyman for the time she was staying there.

On reading down to the small print near the bottom, she began laughing, then almost hysterical at the part that mentioned how if any storage space was needed for large suitcases or muddy boots, an old shack minutes away from the main bungalow would be available. And if visitors wanted somewhere to use as an outdoor office or summer house, for the duration of your stay, then Pedro would be on hand to clear it out and make it habitable as a day retreat.

So we were looking at the garden shed? Serena refused to be cross with herself. It was an easy mistake, and hadn't Broderick thought the same?

Looking out across the bay, she watched colourful yachts and screeching birds that looked distinctly like the gulls back home in St Ives trailing behind a fishing boat heading to the horizon.

But honestly, how could we miss the main house, and end up at the garden shed?

She hit the Reply button and told Rita she'd be moving out as soon as possible, but would honour the two days already booked as the people in the hotel had been really helpful finding her a room at such short notice. There wouldn't be a refund anyway.

Serena wanted to tell her island man

about the silly mistake. They'd forgotten to swap phone numbers, or emails. He hadn't even told her where he lived. She came to her senses.

Of course, married with six kids — maybe four wives for all I know. He was a bit unconventional. Bet he doesn't even have email.

She wondered if he'd turn up to get his money back, but he hadn't seemed worried about that. His generosity was quite rare. Something she'd never come across in anyone — especially after only knowing them for such a short while.

Making her way down to breakfast, Serena walked into the dining room to find a buffet that tantalised her senses. Pineapples with the middles scooped out, filled with chunks of orange, melon and kiwi along with the original pineapple flesh, was on offer for starters. Fish from the bay — freshly caught that morning, the couple on the next table informed her — lay waiting to tempt her taste buds. The aroma of Blue Mountain coffee almost made her swoon with delight. She helped herself to a tropical fruit cocktail and sat down at the table laid for one over by the window.

'Have you any plans?' the petite blonde lady on the next table leaned over to enquire. 'Only we thought we'd take a boat trip, and there are more places if you're interested.'

'I need to go and have a look at somewhere back down the road.' She indicated towards where she should be staying. 'I think I jumped to the wrong conclusion last night. In the confusion I mistook an old shed for my lodgings.'

On any other day, it would have been a good idea. Serena wanted to mix with tourists and locals alike to get as many stories as she could.

She flipped up a picture, and glanced up as more coffee was brought to her table.

'Oh, I still want the two nights here, though — so I can enjoy the facilities a bit longer.' She smiled at the waiter.

'Well, the charming man made sure

you were safe, but if you'd told us the name of your cottage, we might have told you.' The waiter craned his neck to look. 'Ah, over in the next village — looks familiar. Yes, the housekeeper there is a cousin to the owner of this hotel.'

He placed delicious-looking bread and jams on the table, then wafting the serving cloth over his shoulder, continued, 'The trips to see the drunken monkeys go regularly; there are always plenty of boats going over, and to the other islands as well.'

He bustled off with a pile of empty pineapple fruit cups on his tray.

Serena sat up straight, draining her coffee cup.

'Tell you what . . . I'm going over there now, to let them know I've arrived, and then catch a trip later on, say mid-morning or early afternoon. Maybe I'll see you over there?'

The middle-aged couple appeared comfortable together, as if they'd been together for half a lifetime. She had given up on that dream after several short, disastrous relationships. Once boyfriends heard she was a budding journalist, and had half a brain, they ran a mile.

Her career meant a lot to her, and she supposed that being independent financially made her rather a threat to some guys.

Mr and Mrs Purbeck, as they'd told her they were called, were ordering more English breakfast tea. 'We're happy to sit in the conservatory and read for a few hours, and then we can all go together — seeing as we're already friends.'

Serena felt hesitant, but would be glad of the company until she found her bearings.

'If you're certain that's not cramping your style?' She looked at Mr Purbeck to make sure he wasn't just going along with things.

'We haven't got any style to cramp, my dear.' His jolly laugh was reassuring, so she grabbed her haversack and slung it over her shoulder, eager to check out the proper place she should have checked into last night.

'Right . . . Meet you back here in a couple of hours, then, but promise me if you change your mind and want to go on ahead, then you'll carry on, won't you?'

A wafting of hands and the shuffling of crossword books came by way of reply.

★　★　★

How on earth had they missed it? The real Ackee Grove Cottage stood a little way back from the main road. Of course, Broderick had driven around a side road so it was only understandable that they'd found the back entrance and the old shed.

Fancy me thinking that was where I'd be staying. The thought brought a smile to her lips. Lifting her hand to her forehead to shield her eyes from the morning sun, she got a better

36

look at the pink-walled building, with bougainvillea leaves spreading along the side. Lush trees filled the expansive garden. Serena looked forward to finding out their names, and taking pictures.

As she walked cautiously to the front door, a voice from the side of the cottage made her jump.

'Why, hello, there. Welcome to the island. I'm Pedro — come along inside and meet Maria.'

The mellow Caribbean tones were followed by the appearance of a medium-built man, wearing bright patterned shorts and open necked shirt. His handshake was firm and friendly.

'We were expecting you yesterday.' His singsong lilt made her smile. 'We were surprised when you didn't show up. Anyway, you are here now, safe and sound from the looks of it.' He clasped her hands and led the way. 'Come on in, the coffee pot is already on.'

Serena wasn't sure whether to mention she was staying at the hotel for another night, and then decided honesty was the best policy.

'Yesterday we found the back part of the lodgings — err, the other entrance over by the back road . . . ' Putting it into words was almost worse than the shock of finding the old wreck. 'Namely, your shed — and so I thought I'd take another option.' She waited, half-expecting him to fall around laughing, and when he didn't she felt a bit better. 'It had an old signpost dangling in the wind; seeing as we read *Ackee* on the board, I thought that was my lodgings.' *And I've never sounded so stupid in all my life.*

Pedro raised an eyebrow. 'You said *we*. You have company?' He peered round her as if half expecting someone to be following in the rear.

Abruptly she shook her head. 'Oh, a fellow traveller accompanied me. It was handy that he was going my way, a passing ship, you might say.' She hoped it didn't sound as dodgy as it might have done if people didn't know the circumstances.

'Everything is laid on here. Maria will get any shopping you need, and keep an eye on laundry. I'm the handyman and caretaker. We live across the road, but anything you need, give us a call. The door is always open. You'll find we're a friendly community, like one big family. You're not telling me that's your entire luggage?' Pedro looked at her backpack.

'There's another bag, but not lots more.' Serena sat down on the plush sofa and couldn't believe the hideous mistake they'd made. As she sipped yet more delicious coffee, the latest of many since landing on Neptune, she turned to the host who had made her feel so welcome.

'There's another night at the Hotel Atlantis already paid for. Please don't be offended if I stay there for one more night.' Glancing at Pedro, she couldn't imagine him really being offended by anything much at all, with his ready smile and jolly nature.

'Ha ha, Maria . . . Are we offended if our guest has one more night at the Atlantis?'

A woman in a Fifties-style dress, with dark curly hair and a matronly figure, sashayed into the room.

'Hardly, my cousin owns the hotel. But I think you'll really be more comfortable here once you settle in. Now, tell me more about your work. You're a journalist, Pedro tells me?'

Glad to be on a more familiar topic, Serena told the story how she landed the Caribbean trip by chance and intended to make the most of her time here, and relay back some good, original stories for the magazine.

'Drunken monkeys are a bitter-sweet attraction.' Maria laughed. 'The little monkeys — ' she rolled her eyes upward — 'they really are, started getting a taste for it when they gobbled up the fermenting sugar cane and rotting fruit on St Kitts. They were brought over by the slaves — in those days that are gone now, thank goodness

— from West Africa, that's how the story goes. They can be a pain if you want to relax and doze with a drink. On the other hand, they are part of the charm of the islands.' She smiled. 'The best way to get around is by boat, as you would gather.'

Serena drained her coffee cup.

'Yes — that reminds me, I'm going off today with some new friends from the hotel. They're taking a later trip so that I can travel with them.'

She took a mini-tour of the cottage-style bungalow, following Maria as she proudly showed her where everything was. 'I'll be right at home here, I can feel it. Thanks for making me feel so welcome.' She gathered her bag. 'Tomorrow sometime, I'll transfer everything over here. And you can tell me more about the islands — like local recipes, the names of trees in the garden and plants, anything that might be of interest to our readers. If you've got time, that is?'

The couple shared a smiling glance.

41

'You'll come to learn we have all day to sit in the sun and chat. Chill time is from ten in the morning until ten at night. Any work gets done before then. You're in the Caribbean now. Get used to the rhythm of the islands.' Pedro gave a lazy smile. 'Enjoy the boat trip, and don't work too hard. There's always another day for that. Mañana.'

He poured more coffee for himself and Maria, leaving Serena to wonder how anyone ever earned a living if it all got done . . . but not right now.

* * *

'Mind how you step onto the boat.' Mr Purbeck was making sure first his wife, and then Serena, climbed safely aboard. They were all well-equipped with hats and plenty of sunblock.

Serena busied herself taking pictures of the quaint harbour and the many sailing vessels that bobbed on the shimmering water. The boat they were on — Sand Weaver — was equipped to

42

carry up to twenty passengers. A crew of three were on hand. One to steer the boat, another to give a detailed description of dolphins and seals that could be seen if they looked over to the left, and the third crew member strummed a guitar and sang *Kingston Town*. The Caribbean dream had begun. The gentle putter of the boat added to the lazy sunny afternoon.

The school of dolphins came right up the side of the boat and squealed and swooped and dived through the water, sending salty spray cascading over the onlookers who screamed with delight.

All of it was photographed and swiftly noted down with pen and paper by the reporter at large. She'd update the article next time she logged on to her laptop, well away from any exuberant splashing.

Serena snatched more pictures of the enchanting creatures which continued to send showers of spray across those who leaned too far over the edge of the boat. In the tropical temperatures no one minded being drenched in brine, and the tour guide informed them that they could swim with the dolphins if they wanted to.

When they docked in Port Zante Harbour, the sound of reggae music met them, along with wafts of warm coconut and smoked fish aromas that drifted over the sea wall bringing a warm welcome to the passengers.

A buzz of excitement ensued as passengers planned their day, and the crew helped everyone safely disembark. The crew took turns to tell passengers, 'Boats go back to Neptune every two hours, or whatever. We're usually around.' Lots of shoulder-shrugging and head-tilting seemed the norm around these parts.

The laid-back lifestyle was infectious, and it was good to know that if Serena became engrossed in her explorations, they'd be along sometime. A warm breeze brought her more tangy scents of the island and Serena turned her face skyward to feel the warmth and take full advantage of the sunshine. Already, after only one day and using sunblock, she'd noticed her skin and limbs were beginning to take on a bronze glow. The braids kept her hair tidy, and the pink flip flops with an oversized daisy on the front that she'd changed into were really comfortable.

Mr and Mrs Purbeck — John and Jean — followed close behind her. Needing to get out and about on her own but also not wanting to be rude, Serena found herself agreeing to coffee and a light snack when they guided her into a café bistro.

'We need to try local cuisine — oh, it's exciting, isn't it? I've heard we must try the conch fritters.'

Unsure about the conch, Serena opted for a shrimp-stuffed crab. It tasted divine, and from the look on the faces of John and Jean, she was glad she'd said no to their offer. A fruit cocktail drink with the meal was light and refreshing — and as yet, there was not a monkey in sight.

They all ended with a speciality frothy coffee and almond pastries which tasted of heaven. Jean ordered more for on the trip back.

'Look at these! We could go on a bus trip.' Jean placed the pile of leaflets she'd gathered from by the counter onto the table. Her brown curls bobbed as she hitched her chair closer to the table and placed her fancy glasses on to get a better look. One of the brochures showed a stunning beach, in a place called South Friars Bay. More than the exotic scenery and landscape, it was advertising the Shipwreck bar and grill.

John nodded to his wife in approval, and then looked to Serena.

'It would be a good chance to get up close to the monkeys — and look at the colour of that water. In this heat I might even have a swim, and it looks as if there are plenty of activities going on across there. How are you fixed for a bit of surfing, eh, Jeannie?'

46

He peered closely at colourful pictures of surf boards and small boats lined up on the beach. Jean tutted and gave him a playful smack.

After they finished their snack, an open-sided bus picked them up along with a dozen other tourists who were waiting at the bus stop in the square, headed for where the driver told them would be Starfish Bay.

Already, Serena had visions of a silver sandy beach covered in small orange starlike creatures, and she made plans to spend some time writing up an article, a few quick snaps and then get in some swimming and if there was time, relaxing. She was slipping into the sunny Caribbean way of thinking now. *Mañana, there's always tomorrow.*

As the rickety bus with enormous wheels more like a tractor rumbled along the dusty, coastal track, she looked out to sea. Many tiny islands were dotted along the horizon. She wondered if one was where Broderick lived.

Will I even see him again?

Of course not, that would be impossible.

She chided herself for even thinking of such a ridiculous idea. They'd met by chance, and he wasn't overly friendly at the start, but he made up for it in the end with his kindness at the airport and thoughtfulness with giving her a lift, and making sure she was safe in the hotel. He'd certainly gone beyond being helpful.

Kicking herself for not getting more information from him while she had chance, though she knew that had been nigh-on impossible from his closed-off attitude, Serena doodled his name in her notebook. *Broderick Loveday* . . . Quite an unusual name. In fact, it suited him. An eccentric name for the eccentric type of guy he appeared to be.

Serena remembered he'd mentioned a boat man who gave trips. Tapping the end of her pencil on her lips, she decided to ask one of the crew on the way back.

There were so many of the boatmen along the harbour, on Neptune Island. One day she would spend a morning chatting to them. One of them must know him — and if he lived on an island, where did he keep his Jeep? What had he said — Mickey, Nicky? She hadn't written it down, and the name had slipped her mind.

Her thoughts were rudely interrupted when the driver honked the horn of the bus.

'Here we are, ladies and gentlemen. Enjoy Starfish Bay, and I will be along every hour on the hour should you wish to return to the town.'

Giggles and a call of, 'And what if we don't wish to return?' followed.

'Now look at that . . . ' John led the way to the beach. A calypso band with steel drums gave a warm welcome and free cocktails were lined up on the shanty bar. Serena spied a long, furry tail dangling from a nearby palm tree, but after she'd grabbed her camera and whispered to Jean, 'Look — behind you!' she realised it was only an imitation monkey. Hastily she put her camera away, trying not to look like a foolish tourist.

The non-appearance of the little devils was a bit of a let-down, though now she'd be able to relax and plan what to write about next. The calypso band was playing and the singer sang of an island in the sun. For the first time since she'd arrived, work didn't seem quite as important as sampling cocktails. John carried three drinks on a tray. Jean and Serena had already made themselves comfortable on the lounge beds.

'Don't forget the sunblock,' Jean cautioned.

Serena pulled her straw hat down, and covered her limbs in factor thirty, then stowed her notebook and laptop safe under the sun lounger.

'I'm keeping this where I can see it.' She took a sip of the long, tall drink and kept half an eye on the trees behind them. For now, the drunken monkeys must be enjoying the vast array of fruits on offer from the many trees.

Her next assignment, she resolved, would be to interview the members of the calypso band when they took a break, then she'd ask around to find out if there were any animal sanctuaries around these parts. If she wasn't mistaken, that's what Broderick Loveday did for a living — and she needed to thank him properly for helping her out with the hotel.

★ ★ ★

On the Island of Shells, Broderick Loveday gathered enough wood to make a camp fire. The village further inland from where he spent his time, housed no more than fifty in total. He turned to the ocean and felt the warm breeze ruffle his mop of hair. Pushing his fingers through the tangled mass, he knew he'd let himself go, and right at this moment he couldn't care less.

Kathleen didn't want to see him

again, that was clear — and apart from the dent in his ego, he could deal with it. She was never the love of his life, but the hardest part was not being able to see little Aileen. His daughter would grow up not knowing him at this rate. And no matter how much effort he put in to trying to do the right thing, her answer was always the same.

Throwing another log on the camp fire, he settled down on his favourite bench — a tree log — to contemplate his future.

A familiar whistle and the swishing of oars caused him to turn. Agwe, aware of his arrival, steered his boat into the shallows and arrived with enough fish for a supper. He hauled his canoe onto the shore.

'Here's some I caught earlier.'

The wide smile showing off Agwe's gleaming teeth against brown skin along with the familiar Caribbean lilt brought a smile to Broderick's lips.

'The children will be along in a minute.' Agwe smacked Broderick's palm and gripped his hand and feigned the usual arm wrestle they always shared on meeting or leaving. A brief tussle followed, and as usual, Broderick won.

Agwe pointed in playfulness. 'Next time, Brodders. Next time.'

In a matter of minutes, long enough for the two men to get the fish smouldering on the makeshift barbecue, nephews and nieces of Agwe ran barefoot through the shrubbery. The eldest girl carried a basket containing flat breads.

'Mama heard you were back.' She smiled shyly. 'We heard the ferryman talking and saw your smoke signals.' Proudly linking arms with her uncle Agwe, she beamed.

'You'll never arrive on the Island of Shells quietly, no matter how you try. Their mother rustled up a mini-banquet on hearing news of the arrival of the English man.'

Broderick smiled, feeling immediately among family. Why couldn't life always be so simple?

It wasn't long before he was relaxing in his hammock, chatting to Agwe and tucking into his favourite meal. The children had disappeared as quickly as they'd come, seeming to understand that the men wanted to talk, even though they hadn't been told to go.

The simplicity of island life drew him back every time. *Why did I ever think going back to London would make things right?* Being a father was supposed to bring joy and make life wonderful. In his world, Kathleen, the mother of his little girl, only wanted the bright lights. Shopping and being pictured on the front of the latest magazine were her main pleasures.

And she thought I was up for that?

It had taken him the full nine months of her pregnancy to realise that becoming Lady Loveday was her sole aim in life, far more than being married to him. And the way she'd trapped him with the baby news had come as a complete surprise. Enough to put him off the drink, if that was the result of the crazy weekend in the Riviera. So was it any wonder he wanted to escape? She called it running away, and threatened him with not seeing little Aileen if he didn't come back and put a ring on her finger.

Reaching for his book of traditional poems, he turned to the Shakespeare sonnets. He'd made a promise to himself never to cut out Aileen, and always make an effort to see her and keep in touch. Only every time he tried, access was proving more difficult. The latest move was threatening him with going to the press. Kiss and tell, she was talking about. As if anything in any newspaper was ever true.

'You're thinking about your woman back home? How did it go this time? She let you see Aileen?'

Agwe knew the story, but only ever asked once.

He shook his head.

'Still after a ring . . . a great stonking diamond, and a wedding dress and a mansion on a hill.'

Broderick turned to his favourite poem.

> *From fairest creatures we desire increase,*
> *That thereby beauty's rose might never die,*

★ ★ ★

Later, when he was alone, his mind wandered to the girl who had turned up at the decrepit old shack. It made him smile to see her face, horrified at the shanty building. He knew it was part of the bungalow, but thought she'd like a couple of nights of luxury, from the excited way she spoke of her once-in-a-lifetime job opportunity.

He had the money to buy the bungalow, and the hotel, and more besides — one of the drawbacks of being a multi-millionaire — but all he wanted was a quiet life.

Who needed women and families

anyway? But his heart ached for his little Aileen, and he wished things could have turned out differently.

He fell asleep under the stars, resolving that from now on, life would be simple and easy. Days would drift on by and he'd fish, build his fire, read from his poetry book and spend time with Agwe and his extended family.

Life was simple on the island, and that's how he intended to spend the rest of his life. He'd find happiness in keeping busy with making his home just the way he wanted it — no fuss or frills — and any way he could be useful to Agwe and the others would take priority.

The offer of talking through his problems with some shrink had appalled him. Here in his favourite place of all, he would begin to heal from the ghastly materialism that had driven a wedge between himself and the one person in the world he loved with all his heart.

3

Serena pulled her hat down over her face and sipped the frothy pineapple and kiwi cocktail through a straw. A handful of bathers were already in the ocean, and plenty of sun worshippers were taking advantage of the loungers on the beach.

She kept a watchful eye on everything. Even though the newly appointed roving reporter was resting, that didn't mean she wasn't ready to spot an opportunity for a story if it presented itself.

John made his way gingerly over the hot sand. To her right, Jean had her nose in a romantic paperback. Serena enjoyed the sound of the steel drums and wondered if there could be anywhere on earth so idyllic. Surfer dudes made riding the waves look ridiculously easy.

'I think he's considering the surfing experience.' Serena turned to Jean and smiled. Together they watched as John strode deeper into the waves, chatting to one of the lads on the surf boards.

'Why is he waving his arms around so much?' Jean sat up and removed her sunglasses. 'Do you think he's trying to attract attention?'

A small crowd had gathered around John.

Serena was on her feet. 'I'll run and see . . . looks as if they're helping him to the shore.'

Reaching into her bag for light pumps, easier for running in than the fancy flip flops, she laced them up and tore off across the beach to find out what was causing John to perform the jitterbug in Starfish Bay.

'Ow, it's on the top of my foot.' John limped to where one of the surfers had laid a towel down.

'Sit yourself down, Pop. These stings can be nasty, but you stay calm. Help is on its way.'

John looked relieved as Serena approached. She put a hand on his shoulder. 'What happened?'

'They saw a jellyfish.' He looked across to where the surfers were standing close by, staying to offer support. 'It only brushed past, and the blasted thing stung me. I wouldn't mind, but it was a lovely colour and everything. I've never had a sting from one of them before — then again, I'm thinking of our beaches back home. Oww — should have had my plimsolls on, that's what Jean will say.' John tutted and glanced over to where Jean was talking to someone.

'Right, is this serious? Should we be getting him some medical help, do you think? I've done first aid in the office but I can't say a jellyfish sting was on the list of things to look out for.' She scratched her head, and then quizzed the surfers. 'Is it something that needs urgent medical treatment? Should we be getting a doctor in, or taking him to a hospital or something?'

A lad with the matted curls took a closer look.

'Those tentacles will have to be removed, I know that much — hang on.' He shook his damp hair, stuck his fingers under his tongue then raised his head and threw out an almighty whistle, raising his hand to hurry the barman, already making his way towards them, and talking into a large walkie-talkie phone.

Jean was by her husband's side now, and a couple of the calypso band members were taking huge strides in the direction of the patient.

'How do we get them out?' Serena peered at John's foot where a rash and a cluster of the offending tentacles were clearly visible.

'I wouldn't touch them, or you could end up getting stung. We need something like a razor shell, which might do it.' Eagerly the surfer and his pals searched the beach.

'Tweezers! In my make-up bag. Stay still.' The instruction to John was met with an ironic stare. 'I'll be right back.'

Tearing across the beach, Serena hoped someone would find a suitable shell, but it wouldn't be half as good as the grippers she had in her bag. Fumbling and then deciding to take the whole lot, she scarpered back across the sand.

By now a crowd had gathered around John, all telling him to hold on, and help was coming. One of the calypso men was carrying a small case with a cross on the side. Of course, they'd be prepared. She wondered whether to stand back and let them proceed without her help.

'So, you got them?' a dark-skinned man enquired, looking quizzically at her make-up bag covered in a lipstick print design.

'Of course, they're in here.' She tipped the contents onto the sand. Normally she was quite protective of her make-up collection, but today, her friend was in agony from the sounds he was making and Jean was hysterical with worry.

'Everybody, stand back please.' Gripping the tweezers, Serena aimed for the tentacles, tiny hair-like structures, protruding from John's foot.

'Make sure they come out in one go. They'll be more trouble if you don't take every bit out.' The man with the first aid bag was dabbing something onto a pad of cotton wool. 'You'll need to hurry — unless you want me to?'

Shaking her head, Serena wanted to do this herself. She looked at John. 'You OK?'

He nodded. Serena gave a tiny shudder and hoped the obtrusions would come out in one piece. She did have a first aider certificate but she was hardly a nurse. The most she'd ever had to do was to stick a plaster on Alyn Carter's thumb when he'd got a paper cut.

That was before her lucky break as the roving reporter — but she certainly hadn't bargained on treating her new friend for jellyfish stings.

With a slightly trembling hand, she

grasped the tweezers, took a tentacle between the pointed ends and gripped firmly. 'Hold still, John, whatever you do.' A brief glance to check he was going to stay still, and she firmly and slowly tugged.

Aware of the voices telling her not to touch any of the tentacle, she handed the small tweezers to the man who stood closest to her.

He disposed quickly of the stinger and handed them back. 'Same again, keep up the good work.' His grin was encouraging, and Serena proceeded to tug at each nasty little tentacle in turn until John sighed and rubbed his hand over his face.

'Is that it — can I stand up now?'

Jean was crouched by his side.

'Sit still, love — listen to what they tell you. I'm worried he might go into shock.' She looked to where the first aider was placing a wad of cotton wool over the red blotches on his foot. 'Do you serve tea at the bar?'

Serena stood back and watched while

they dressed the wounds, and taped a cotton wool pad to the foot with gauze. She noticed the bar man was nodding in answer to Jean's question.

'English breakfast, will that do? You can have it with milk or a slice of lemon.'

'Consider it done.' Serena turned and jogged off to the log cabin-style bar. If there was something she could do to help the lovely couple who'd taken to her from the start, it was to brew a pot of tea. She found a stainless steel pot, milk and sugar in pots, and chunky mugs under the counter. She knew John and Jean took milk and sugar, on the weak side. She prepared them each a drink and then glancing up, saw some of the bar workers approaching.

While the kettle boiled, she reached for her purse. 'I'll pay for this. They've been treating me to everything so far today.' She tried hard to smile, but the tension of the last half an hour was suddenly taking a grip. An overwhelming tiredness hit her between the eyes.

'You must be joking. Tell me you aren't serious please?' The Caribbean man with the palm tree shirt and cut off shorts to match looked as shocked if she'd told him she was stealing the entire contents of his shack. 'On the house — this is an emergency. He's got some astringent on there now and he'll be fine. Take a tray from that shelf behind you.' He gestured to a stack of vintage trays embellished with grapes and bottles of wine. 'Let me help.'

Placing the pot and mugs, milk and sugar onto the tray, he carried it across to the table between the loungers where not so long ago, they were enjoying a relaxing afternoon.

Hobbling with support from the surfer guys who kept asking if he was feeling all right, John made his way back along the beach, with Jean fussing beside them.

'All right if we put you down here then, mate?'

The surfers made sure he was comfortable on a beach chair before leaving him to his tea.

Jean handed the make-up bag to Serena.

'They said it would be best to throw your tweezers away, love, sorry about that.' She flopped down onto a chair and saw the tea laid out. 'Have I ever seen such a sight? They say he'll be all right, but to keep an eye out for a delayed reaction. Will you help me keep an eye on him? Only you could see something I might miss.'

'Of course, my pleasure.' Serena poured the tea, only sorry she hadn't added a third cup. Enjoy the drink — and I think I'll join you, actually.'

She left them sipping English breakfast tea, while she went to ask for another mug. The three enjoyed a welcome mug of tea and unanimously agreed it reminded them of home. They'd formed a friendship that each felt would be a lasting one.

Gathering the empty tea things onto

the tray, Serena stood up to take it back to the bar.

'That's better.' Jean looked happier and made a complete fuss of John until he told her to get back to the romantic book.

'You know how I like to make sure you're all right — and no going back in the water. That's unless you wear something on your feet, and leave your shorts on and . . . '

Not able to hide her smile, Serena left them to what seemed to be normal chatter and returned the tea things, and then wandered over to where a group of locals laughed and chatted.

'Care to join us, lady of the moment?' One of the calypso players welcomed her by pulling up an extra chair. 'That was swift work back there — we know who to call on if we get stung.'

She heard a jokey comment, 'Let's go and get stung quickly.' She'd only been here a short while, but the warmth of the locals was endearing.

'If you hadn't moved quickly like you did, we might have called on the man of the island.'

'Which man?' For a moment, she wondered if they were speaking about Broderick. With all the commotion, he'd completely gone from her mind.

'Yeah, that's right, the Witch Doctor. He would have mixed some herbal potion and your friend would have had the magic touch from Jaheim, our local medicine man.'

'Jaheim . . . He lives here on the island?' Serena had to know more. 'No, wait. You're winding me up, right?' They might be teasing the quaint little English girl, she realised. 'There aren't any witch doctors these days; it's a tourist myth, I guess.'

She accepted a pineapple cocktail from the tray and the bar man told her, 'No myth, beautiful lady with braided hair. Jaheim will make any magic you need. If you require a love spell, or a healing poultice,' he glanced across to where John was laughing and almost over his ordeal. 'Say you wanted to find a lost relative, start a family, he's the one to ask.'

'He lives near here?'

I mustn't sound too eager, as if I really want anything like a spell or lotion or potion. But it wouldn't hurt to pay him a visit. Wonder if John and Jean would be up for that tomorrow?

4

You don't have to come; only I thought it would be an adventure.' Serena gave John an encouraging smile; he looked unsure.

'I don't want to spoil the fun, only we should find out a bit more about this, er, Witch Doctor before we go?' John threw Jean a dubious glance. 'Perhaps I've watched too many spy films. I don't want to end up in the cooking pot — wouldn't make for good holiday snaps, would it?'

The bus transporting them back to the harbour bounced as they hit a pot hole, throwing them all to the right, then left of the bus.

'For crying out loud, it's like being in a tumble dryer,' John gasped and they all clung on to the rail of the seat in front; white knuckles were showing. It wasn't unlike the snake-train at the

71

Safari Park Serena visited last summer.

'I've had enough excitement for today, and probably to last me all week from the way this foot is stinging.' John had his mini moan, then spent the next fifteen minutes convincing Jean he didn't need further assistance and told her he was only feeling slightly sorry for himself.

Serena smiled as the bus driver took a sharp bend a bit fast and they were all thrown first left then right. Jean spoke cheerily.

'How about we get over today's excitement, and get back across to Neptune on the ferry first? Then later, we can settle down and have a good old natter over a glass of wine. Mull over the pros and cons of it all. Calling on a Witch Doctor isn't something we have to rush into, but I'm not saying no.' She winked at Serena. 'When we've had chance to think it over, then we can decide.'

Serena nodded, sat back and closed her eyes.

It might be best if I went alone; it's really not fair to expect them to traipse around the island looking for the magic man. I shouldn't have even asked them if they wanted to come.

As if she'd tuned in to her thoughts, Jean scolded, 'Don't you dare go exploring in the jungle, looking for a voodoo man without us. Promise me we'll talk about it first. Now then, anyone want some of those mixed nuts I bought from the beach café?' She reached for the bag of loose nuts at the same moment the bus turned another hairpin bend. The contents of the bag went flying, scattering a mixture of Brazils, almonds and pecans under the seats.

The evening had turned deliciously cooler and Serena took the short walk down to the harbour, enjoying the tranquil evening, glad to be alone with her thoughts. The Island by night looked even more magical and the tinkling wind chimes gave out an otherworldly charm. The water front was still busy with tourists mingling and the boat men chatting to one another about their day.

Their laughter carried across the breeze and Serena wondered how it would be to have such a carefree job, in a place so peaceful, yet full of colour and life all at the same time.

The seafront rippled with a silver glow from the rising moon, and strings of coloured lights bobbed in the gentle breeze. Already tables were filling up with couples ordering fish dishes alongside carafes of wine and exotic-looking Margaritas.

A gentle rhythm of reggae music surrounded the boardwalk and silhouettes of late ferry boats gently bumped up against the harbour wall adding to the magic. She sat on the edge of the breakwater and pulled her feet up underneath her, tucking her full skirt around her knees. Breathing in the salty air, she forgot for a moment all about reports and stories for back home, and soaked up the atmosphere of the

Caribbean evening.

Being on her own was a life choice she'd made, but when she glimpsed to her right, and spotted yet another couple taking a table for two she forced herself to ignore the unexpected pang of jealousy that hit somewhere just below her ribcage. Would she ever find herself in a position where she'd have to compromise and go along with another person's wishes?

Hardly — I've finally stepped on the first rung of the ladder to the career I've always wanted. Who needs that candlelit supper nonsense anyway?

Music and laughter filled the cosy harbour and she forced herself to stop feeling like the only singleton in the village and get among people and find out more about the nightlife on the small waterfront of Neptune Island.

She walked along to where a sign *Fisherman's Creek* dangled from white rope. She chose that particular bar as she'd seen some of the ferrymen going in earlier. It looked more local than some of the more tourist-type pubs, though she did spot a couple of the other residents from her hotel sitting outside. She smiled to acknowledge them as she walked past.

Serena ordered a pear cider and found a high stool by the end of the bar. She sipped her drink, glad when one of the ferry men over by the window called out and waved her over.

'Hey, pretty lady, come and join us. Nobody visits Neptune and spends time alone. We make everyone welcome. Don't worry, we're only friendly — no Shirley Valentines around here.'

It made her laugh to think he might be comparing her to the middle-aged housewife who ran away to Greece in that old film. Her aunt and grandma used to watch it and drink wine and eat chocolate while dreaming of an escape that they knew was all in fun.

The bar was filling up. Other guests from her hotel were nearby, also chatting to the ferry men.

He guided her towards a table where

a group of locals were mulling over their working day. Donny, he told her his name was, pulled out a chair and gestured that she be seated. He left and soon returned with a tray full of drinks.

More people joined them — ferrymen mostly, and a couple of teenagers whom she imagined might be children of one of the workers.

'You want something to eat?' Donny asked and all eyes focused her way as she reached out for a bottle of cola.

Serena shook her head. 'No thank you, you're more than kind, the drink is perfect.' Listening to the conversation that struck up again, she gathered that they mostly drank non-alcoholic drinks, as their working day began any time someone wanted to go anywhere in a ferry boat.

Happily sipping her drink, Serena listened to their chatter, and then she heard the name. She sat perfectly still and listened.

'I'm telling you, that's your problem, Nicky.' She couldn't help smile at the sing-song lilt to the voice. 'There are not enough hours in your day. I swear you'd take someone out now if they asked you to. You're married to that yacht, man.' Laughter followed.

That was it! The name of the ferry man . . . He'd said, *find Nicky — say Brodders sent you*. It had to be him. How many boat men going by the name of Nicky could there be along the waterfront?

She waited her chance until there was a break in the conversation. She leaned towards the man they'd been calling Nicky and said in her best journalist voice, 'You know a man named Brodders?' She felt herself colouring slightly. 'I know him as Broderick. A man with a beard, and . . . well . . . thing is, I only met him on the flight over. He told me to ask for a boatman called Nicky.'

She looked towards the man in the striped T-shirt and hoped she hadn't made a complete fool of herself. It wouldn't be the first time. 'You'd be able to take me around the small islands?'

Why am I acting like an idiot at the mention of the scruffy old tramp who's probably glad to be back on his own patch?

She took hold of the situation. 'I don't know him that well, only I wanted to thank him for being kind to me.' It didn't matter either way — only as she was among the ferrymen, she might as well mention it. 'You know where he lives?'

Shut up, Serena . . . no need to elaborate . . . they don't need to know he bought coffee, gave me a lift and booked me into a hotel. And who cares where he lives?

'Aw, yeah, you mean the recluse. He landed on the island over there when he fell overboard from the cruise liner.' Nicky nodded in what Serena guessed might be a southerly direction. 'Stayed for a good while . . . he wouldn't have gone back, only he had news from home. The real Robinson Crusoe, he is.

He wouldn't want you to visit. You know that saying, *No man is an island*?'

She nodded.

'Well — he is. But my yacht sails any time after six o'clock in the morning, if you want to go anywhere else.'

★ ★ ★

She looked across the sea, where the reflection of the low moon trailed like thread across navy water. Only the sound of lapping waves against the harbour wall broke into her thoughts. Her drink bottle was almost empty — she'd told the boatmen she would let them know when she wanted ferrying to the other islands. It was time to get some articles written and pictures sent back, otherwise her editor Rita would start wondering what she was doing.

What news had made him leave so suddenly? And surely if he told her to talk to Nicky, he wouldn't be that surprised if she rocked up on a beach near to where he was staying one day?

She finished her drink and placed the empty bottle on a nearby table. She wanted to get back to the hotel. This would be her last night there, and she intended to get a good night's sleep after what had turned out to be an eventful day. For tomorrow, the monkeys might await her — and the witch doctor as well.

She waved to the boatmen and thanked them for the drink with a thumbs-up sign.

Glad to be on speaking terms with him, she would ask Nicky if he could take her around in his yacht tomorrow; if on the offchance she stumbled on the island where that eccentric Englishman who went by the name of Brodders happened to hang out, she'd be able to thank him properly. He would play a key role in getting to the drunken monkeys as well. She felt sure of that.

★ ★ ★

81

Serena needed to move into Ackee Grove cottage, since her company had been kind enough to provide her with personal accommodation, with help thrown in for good measure. She gathered her few belongings next morning after an early breakfast and then said her goodbye for now, to everyone at the Atlantis Hotel.

'We must keep in touch.' Jean gave Serena a motherly hug. 'And we will go and see the Witch Doctor with you. I'm really interested in alternative medicine; maybe he could help with something for John's foot.' She smiled.

'That's along the lines of what I had in mind.' Serena nodded and looked to where John had his shoe off and a woollen sock covering the offending wound. 'Does it still sting much?'

He made a balancing gesture with his hand. 'Mm, fifty-fifty. The sock makes it feel better. I'll not be swimming barefoot from now on, though.'

Somehow, Serena had the feeling that he liked to make a bit of a fuss, and

82

Jean was making sure he had everything he needed. A more traditional couple than these two would be hard to find.

'Well, as long as you're able to get about, we could go towards the end of the week. I've been chatting to the ferrymen, and we can hire a boat and make a day of it, rather than go on a bigger boat full of strangers. It's easy to make friends in a small place, isn't it?'

Leaving them gathering the daily crossword, and plumping up cushions in the huge conservatory, where they would soon be drinking coffee and asking for biscuits to go with it, she took the short journey to Ackee Grove and found Pedro and Maria busy in the garden.

His face lit up and he called out. 'You've decided to join us! Just when I was about to get some shopping in. Have you eaten? Only there are fresh eggs.'

The squawk of what sounded like a chicken fight about to start, greeted her as Pedro fished around in the nesting box. 'Look at that — did you ever see such fresh eggs?'

Serena shook her head. Even though she lived in a rural area, she mostly bought eggs from the supermarket — always free range, but they'd never be as free range as these offerings in front of her.

'I've never seen eggs so speckled and huge,' she gasped. 'And yes, I had breakfast at the hotel, thanks. Actually . . . I've got some exploring to do today. I'm officially at work, so don't feel you have to be on duty as such.'

She bit her lip, hoping they wouldn't be offended. It was good to have a handyman and cook available, but she really wanted to get going with the photos and articles. 'I might be away for a good while, I'm not sure yet.' She glanced from Maria to Pedro, and felt relieved to see they understood.

'Hey, we're around most mornings, but you come and go as you please. If you need anything, our number is on the pad in the kitchen. We always leave the key under the silver milk churn by the front door if we're not here. Now if you don't mind, I have a vegetable plot to tend to.' He walked off down the rambling garden, whistling.

Serena saw Maria, kneading a mound of dough on the worktop. She hoped they weren't going to all this trouble just for her.

'I'm going to be out a lot — please don't cook just for me,' she said apologetically.

'It's only there if you need it, and it will be eaten sooner or later. I could make you a sandwich if you like? There's roast chicken in the fridge. We always keep fresh bread and cold meat to go with the salads.' She glanced out to where Pedro worked his hoe steadily over the veggie patch.

Lifting the lid on the bin marked *BREAD*, she fished out a cottage loaf.

'One I prepared earlier.' She waved the plump bread and began to slice it.

In a jiff, she'd wrapped a pile of sandwiches and added some fruit to a striped bag. 'Take these with you, and enjoy a taste of our island when you stop for a break.'

★ ★ ★

Nicky had just left, the others told her when she reached the harbour. Drat, and just when she thought it was all going smoothly.

'Well, that's a shame, I really wanted to explore some of the smaller islands.'

'You want to see some beautiful places to write home about?' The young man smiled and his teeth gleamed against dark skin. 'Come aboard, you can catch a ride with Nicky another day. I only paddle slowly, it's a calm sea — and you mentioned your friend the castaway man.'

She glanced along the row of waiting sailing vessels. Some catered for groups, others were smaller, and here was one ready to go. Glancing behind to check the board for prices and times of departure, she heard the young man's laughter.

'Don't bother with that . . . it's only for tourists. You're local, we know you already. It's only a few dollars, and you can settle at the end of the week, or next week, whenever.'

He waved a hand as if it didn't matter to him whether she paid at all. All this carefree, laid-back style was quite refreshing.

She pulled out her notebook and scribbled down the date. 'Here. *IOU. 1 ferry ride. Signed, S. Winter.*' She tore the page and handed it to him. 'Only on condition that you let me know exactly how much it will be by the time we come back. Oh — you do return trips, I presume?'

He flashed that wide grin again, revealing a set of perfect white teeth that many of her friends back home would pay a fortune for at the dentist. 'Of course, madam — now please be seated and enjoy your trip across the

Caribbean Sea. My name is Daniel.' He gave her another smile as he set off across the water.

She settled back and watched the waves rippling to the shore. White horses in the distance pranced in a row. Palm trees waved in the warm breeze and Serena wondered if life could get more perfect. The boatman gave a mention now and then as to the direction they were headed.

'You mentioned the Island of Shells.'

'I did?' Serena gave a frown, not sure whether he was mistaken or not.

'Robinson Crusoe's island. He landed there after the accident. He hardly ever leaves.'

In the distance, a typical island covered with palm trees, like the one she imagined they spoke about on *Desert Island Discs*, came into view. Suddenly she had a mini panic. What if he was back to being the moody man on the plane?

Now Daniel was looking to his right with a worried frown.

'Aw, man, and just when I have a tourist on board. Grab the life-jacket and put it on . . . now.' He turned his boat around and told her to lie low.

All Serena could hear was a sound like a motor boat coming closer, moving pretty quickly.

'Bloody pretend pirates, kids playing at scaring the holidaymakers. Don't worry. You'll be all right; you're not carrying anything important, are you?'

'What? Apart from my laptop and camera and other things, you mean?' Irritated by his flippant remark, Serena wished she'd waited for Nicky, as Broderick had told her. She knew they weren't far from his home and trouble was approaching, from the worried catch in Daniel's voice.

The speed boat circled the ferry boat and the teenagers cried out. 'You need a quicker route to where you're going?' They targeted Serena and pulled up alongside the boat. 'We can do a cheaper price than him.' They jeered at Daniel and began to rock the boat. Serena was feeling more afraid by the second.

'No, thank you. I'm fine here, thanks for asking.' She acted braver than she felt and made sure the buckles on her life jacket were fastened properly, in case she needed to swim to the nearest shore in a hurry.

'Don't forget, if you need a quicker method of transport, we're the Caribbean Buccaneers. Shami and Rhawand, that's us.' The taller of the two youths threw a business card at Serena and looked at her bag with a little too much interest.

She knew she'd need to start being more careful who she got talking to — and suddenly the idea of travelling alone in a strange place wasn't as appealing as she first thought.

5

'Caribbean Buccaneers? I've heard of the Pirates of the Caribbean, but I didn't really want to meet any.' Serena sat up and breathed properly at last. 'D'you think they'll come back, or what?'

The aqua waters of the tropics had become a lot more sinister and held more danger than she'd bargained for.

'And as well as stinging jellyfish, are there crocodiles in there?' She glanced down into the water and searched the surface, checking for any killer sharks or stingray-type fish.

Daniel gave a bemused frown.

'You're not in Miami, and we're in the ocean, not on swampland. You English sure are funny. No wonder they call you eccentric, with your books and pens and worrying all the time.' He looked back in the direction of where the speedboat had sped off leaving a torrent of surf in its wake.

'You think they'll come back, don't you?'

She tried to keep the panic from her voice, and held on tightly to her belongings.

'Hardly . . . like I told you, they're kids, but the danger is that they're the scouts.' He looked at her with huge whites in his dark eyes.

'I'm guessing you don't mean like Boy Scouts?' Serena took a slow breath and scanned the water. An island loomed not far ahead.

'More like the kind of scouts the ants send out. If the scout returns, they know it's safe; if not, they send another scout. They're the lookout boys. We need to land on an island — and sooner rather than later, before they inform the Blackeye Wanderers.' He gave her a warning look and stressed, 'Don't ask. There are some things you really don't need to know.'

Serena was thankful that the roaming

Buccaneers didn't put in another appearance and she felt her heart rate drop slightly as he manoeuvred the boat alongside a wooden jetty that jutted out from some reeds and trailing trees that looked like willows dangling into the water.

Hastily scrambling onto the rickety landing station, she couldn't get out of the craft quickly enough. She turned to watch him secure his boat.

'So who are The Blackeye Wanderers?'

Not entirely sure she really wanted to know, the curiosity of her journalistic mind got the better of her. And it would be better to be forewarned if some unsavoury gang were after her.

'You seriously didn't think you could go roaming around the Caribbean, especially in the middle of the smaller mostly un-named islands without coming across a pirate ship or two, did you?' His grin belied the threatening tone of his words. 'Listen — where you come from, is it in the city? And you have the bad guys, right?'

She nodded quietly, not wanting to let him know she came from a small seaside town on the Cornish coast — nor interrupt his conversation.

'Same goes for the seas. There's always the Blackeye Boys, only it's kept quiet otherwise tourists would never come and stay in this area.' He tilted his head and assured her that the pirates of the Caribbean were no myth. 'The sandy part of the beach is over on the other side, it's hidden mostly from passers-by. Come on, I'll show you, and I can smell a campfire. There might be some form of human life around.'

As they were talking, a group of children had appeared, looking as if they might be little tree urchins. Most had bare feet and bronzed limbs, the girls' hair tied in braids like her own, and the boys wore shy smiles as they peered at the new arrivals on their island.

'Hello.' Serena spoke gently as she didn't want to frighten them, but the children looked more curious than afraid.

Suddenly a shower of large round objects began to thud to the ground. High up above them, the rustle of leaves and then a warlike cry of 'Bombs away!' sounded out around the shrubbery.

A man shimmied down the tree, and landed with a light jump in front of them.

'Hello there! I'm Agwe — you sight-seeing, or here for a purpose?'

The children were filling baskets with the fruit, setting up a chant of 'Paw paw pie for supper.'

The boatman spoke to Agwe, and then a rustle in the trees drew their attention. The branches of a huge lime tree were pushed to one side and a familiar hairy beard and shaggy mop appeared.

'Oh, we're only here to do a bit of sightseeing,' Serena answered the islander's question then turned and gave a wide-eyed smile to the man she felt she'd known for far more than a day.

'Hello again, Broderick. Fancy us landing on the very island where you live! You'll never believe what happened on the journey over. I've never been so scared in all my life.'

She made her way towards him.

'You! Why did you come over here? I told you, it's the commercial hotspots you want if you're looking for drunken monkeys.'

Immediately a ripple of laughter sounded out from the little ones.

'That's what Mam calls you two when you've been drinking the palm wine.' The eldest girl clasped Agwe's hand and gazed up at her father adoringly as she and the others listened in.

'We had an inspection from the Buccaneer boys. I need to be on my way — unless there's a brew on offer?' The boatman looked towards Agwe, who led him to a pack of supplies and began to open a flask. He waved the children away to go find what might be left of the picnic.

Broderick was frowning and not acting as if he was at all pleased to see her. She'd risked all her equipment and probably her life to get here — only to be met with the grumpy bloke from the plane.

'I told you to ask for Nicky if you ventured out on the waters on your own. You can't begin to know what dangers lurk around here — otherwise you'd have stayed around the busy ports.'

His annoyance was apparent.

'I only wanted to thank you for paying for the hotel. It was a real touch of luxury. You were so kind. I'll be going as soon as Daniel's had some refreshments.'

She glanced round to see if the man taking her on the return trip was ready.

'Oh, no, you don't — not if you want to get your work done. You might be the roaming reporter, but the way you're going about things, you'll be sending pictures back from the bottom of the

Caribbean.' He parted the trees and took her arm to lead her through to a pathway.

'I brought some food, from the cottage. And you'll never guess — ' When she told him about the shanty shack, and how it was the garden shed, he only smiled.

In a clearing not far away, a camp fire smouldered. 'There's a sandy beach over this way,' Broderick said. He led the way up a small grassy hill and through some shrubbery. Serena wondered what the berries were and if she could eat them, but didn't ask as she'd made enough blunders for today to last a week.

The beach was a curve of golden sand, just like in a travel brochure, yet she didn't feel the urge to get her camera out just yet. She only wanted to admire the view. Not a building or tourist in sight. Only the sound of the waves, with a faraway echo of sea birds in flight, surrounded her. Breathing in the blissful moment, wishing it could last forever, Serena felt a whisper of a breeze on her cheeks.

'Now I see why you like coming here.' She turned to Broderick, watching the seashore.

'It's home to me. There's nowhere I'd rather be.' His smile told her he wasn't being whimsical — he meant it.

They sat on the grassy bank on the edge of the beach watching the waves lap against the sand, sharing the sandwiches Maria had made earlier.

'Let me show you some wild garlic, and other herbs . . . we sprinkle them on the barbecue.'

He parted the shrubbery and pointed out small plants and odd-shaped fruits and berries growing from vines.

'I think that's an aubergine — it looks like the ones in the supermarket.' Immediately she'd said it, Serena felt like a complete tourist.

He didn't mock; only told her they were known by the name of Boulanger in the Caribbean. There were cucumber-type fruits growing from a vine, and she helped him to collect a variety of fruits or salads, she wasn't sure which category they'd come under, but whatever they were, it looked a colourful assortment of snacks. And all for free.

'I'll show you how I make the marinade for the fish supper, if you'd like to watch?'

Serena nodded. Every bit of information she could learn and take back with her or use another time was useful. And he made it look so easy, chopping with his penknife, reminding her of a proper survival expert.

'Limes give it the zest that I like, and plenty of colour as well.' He handed her a piece of fruit.

Later in the day, Broderick made a space for her to sit on the huge log which was tipped on its side. Seemingly this was his sofa, and it felt a lot more comfortable than it looked.

'You'll have to stay here tonight; it's not safe to go back on that small boat.' He didn't look at her, and stared into the fire as he spoke. 'I'll get word over to Nicky and he'll be the one who can take you back.'

'Get word?' She turned, studying him for the first time since they'd parted on the first day she arrived. 'You have email? Or were you going to use Skype? Ah, no, I've got it; you'll send smoke signals, like in the cowboy movies.'

He wasn't laughing, and Serena wondered what on earth she'd got herself into.

6

'Did you just ask me to stay overnight on the island?' Serena pulled a stern face and pursed her lips, though in reality she felt a warm ripple running through her — she felt safer with the wild man than the boat man.

She couldn't hide the fact that she was pleased, and gave herself a mental ticking-off.

What's got into you, Serena Winter? When did you start going off with strange men? Here in the space of a few days it's happened twice.

'Where did Daniel go . . . the one who ferried me across?' Serena didn't relish the thought of a repeat crossing, but at the same time she didn't want to go all gushy on Broderick, saying, *Thank you so much for saving my life* . . . That would be just too dramatic, and those boys were probably

102

only tearaways having a bit of fun at her expense.

'You don't need to worry. Agwe will look after him back at the village.' He stood up, walked over to where a khaki hammock was strung low between two trees, and lifted a huge book. 'This is the item I can't be without — my poetry book. You know, like on *Desert Island Discs*?'

He made his way back to the log and sat down by her side. He opened the huge book and turned to a page that was folded over at the top corner.

He glanced towards Serena, as if checking she was still listening — or maybe he was wondering whether she might be laughing at him. She wasn't. He quoted from the book.

'*There is a pleasure in the pathless woods,*
There is a rapture on the lonely shore,
There is society, where none intrudes,

*By the deep sea, and music in its
    roar:
I love not man the less, but nature
    more.*
'Lord Byron, from *Childe Harold's
Pilgrimage.*'

The poetry reading provided a moment of calm which Serena found a welcome change after an eventful couple of days. She drew a deep breath; she was on a tropical island in the middle of the Caribbean Sea, listening to an eccentric English man reading from a treasured book of poems. From the look on his face, and the tone of his voice, he was living every word.

Now there's a man who would be good on stage, she thought.

'Have you done any acting? You prefer being alone, I see that . . . you read with such feeling.'

For the first time since she'd met this sultry man on the plane, he appeared more vulnerable and the moody edge was disappearing. Clearly the poetry meant a lot to him. At first Serena felt he was trying to convey the message that he wished she would leave him alone, then realised he'd read about not thinking less of man — or woman — but loving nature more. A bit like Bear Grylls — though she still thought he was more of a Robinson Crusoe than a bear.

His evident appreciation of literature belied his scruffy appearance. The unkempt beard covered half of his face, and she imagined he might use it to hide behind, given his reclusive tendencies. She felt almost a sisterly warmth towards him — he had been kind and generous and was now revealing a little more of himself. Like in an exclusive interview . . . She really needed to be getting more stories sent back to the magazine.

A rustle in the shrubbery behind them broke into her thoughts before she had time to ask him any more questions.

'May we join you?' It was Agwe and

the ferry man, Daniel. 'It's party time in the village, and we wanted some quiet so we can talk. About things like when it's the best time to cross the water. We're thinking sometime tomorrow, say after mid-morning.' They both nodded to Serena.

'Pull up a log.' Broderick turned a page of the gargantuan volume, which she realised contained work by multiple poets. He now began a second reading, telling them this one came from Robert Louis Stevenson's *The Vagabond*, written in 1896 . . .

> *Give to me the life I love,*
> *Let the lave go by me,*
> *Give the jolly heaven above*
> *And the byway nigh me,*
> *Bed in the bush with stars to see,*
> *Bread I dip in the river-*
> *There's the life for a man like me,*
> *There's the life forever.*

Growing deliciously sleepier by the minute, Serena listened to more poetry readings from Broderick, and then a series of traditional Caribbean stories told by Agwe with the sound of crickets and frogs as background. She thought that everyone should have a chance to feel such peacefulness.

It was a far better way to get high than spending a fortune on expensive wine or drugs. Not that she'd tried the latter, but the warmth from the fire and pleasant company had given her a rosy glow, and tingling from her head right down to her toes. A feeling she'd never experienced before . . . and she liked it quite a lot.

'There's fish for us all . . . ' Broderick spoke softly as he put together a cooking rack and placed the large chunks of fish he'd caught on top of it, close enough to the smouldering charcoal of the fire without catching light. He'd shown her earlier how to prepare the herbs, cucumber and wild garlic. He mixed in spices he already had in pots, black pepper and sea salt, making a combination of wild thyme and limes, using the juice and chopped lime rind to baste the fish.

He gently lifted the fish from the griddle with a thin piece of wood, and rolled the pieces into the marinade mixture on a flat plate. Returning them to the fire, he reached for another plate, the kind used for camping. Onto that one he tipped a dusting of flour, and more spices. Quickly once again he removed the fish from the cooking grid and rolled it through the thin layer of flour to coat it completely. He returned the fish to the fire and sat back to listen to the rest of the story.

Agwe was telling of that famous night he'd caught rum smugglers. The story went that they insisted they were carrying dead bodies in the huge coffin-like boxes on a sailing boat.

'And when the Chief Commissioner asked what the unfortunate people had died from, can I tell you what they said?' He looked round at his captive audience.

'What did they say?' Broderick asked.

'Let me guess . . . snake bites?'

'No, he said there'd been an outbreak of cholera. And not wanting to get closer in case of infection, they escaped with the lot . . . that's until they were followed and had a little surprise waiting for them when they docked in over Florida Keys. And, when it all came out, they were a band of females. Can you believe it — lady pirates?' Agwe was talking to Daniel now.

'Didn't they sound like females when they spoke?' Broderick quizzed him.

'How do I know? They'd supplied me with so much rum it was hard to see straight.' Laughter rippled around the gathering and Serena felt safe among friends.

There was nothing about Broderick that made her feel wary or unsure. If any other man she'd recently met had told her she needed to stay with him, outdoors for the night, she'd have probably screamed and called the police, or in no uncertain terms, told him where to get off. Of course it might take time for a police motor boat to shimmy across the waves — if it didn't get accosted by a wannabe pirate boat on the way.

No — she trusted him. She was good at knowing when someone was genuine or not.

He was a dominant force; even sitting on a log on an island, reading romantic poetry, he looked like a man who could stick up for himself.

For all his moodiness, Broderick was far more mature than other men she'd met. She really hadn't had a proper boyfriend — just dates that never led to anything. Broderick had looked out for her so far, so she should relax . . . but she was wondering where she was going to sleep.

The smoked fish simply melted in her mouth, and tasted like something from heaven. The mixture of wild herbs and lime with the spices made it feel as if sparklers were going off inside her mouth. If this was life on a Caribbean island, she wanted more. She was energised, her drowsiness forgotten.

'We'll get back to the village, and catch you tomorrow.' The ferryman spoke to Serena. 'There's a few of us going across to Neptune, and it'll be just after lunch, so no hurry.'

Agwe gave Broderick the same mixture of arm wrestle and grip to say goodbye. It looked like a brotherly, macho handshake, and she could see how much they respected each other.

So now she was alone with her own Robinson Crusoe.

'I don't suppose you can get Wi-Fi here?' She hesitated to ask; he'd probably be disgusted after the poetry and folk stories, but even so . . .

'Come with me.' He picked up the crockery that lay around the camp fire from the fish supper and piled them up in a bowl.

'If you're taking those to wash, then you must let me do it. There's so much to learn about living on an island. And don't be mad at me for asking, you know, about the Wi-Fi.'

He looked slightly amused. 'Now why am I not surprised one bit at you needing your communication with the outside world?' Raising his eyes skyward, he succeeded in making her feel like a proper townie. Yet she wasn't really.

He threw a cloth over his shoulder and led the way through the trees.

★ ★ ★

They walked for what felt like ages, yet it was only quarter of an hour when she checked her watch. He led her up a grassy hill, which would have felt steep to her at one time — but having been walking on the drunken monkey island, and on Neptune more than she normally would have, she could easily manage the gradual ascent to the summit.

The view from the top took her breath away. As far as she could see, small islands dotted the ocean, distant miniature palm trees swayed, and the

112

rippling waters almost sang to her. She could quite easily be in a magical wonderland, and the freshness of the salty air made her skin tingle.

'You'll need to pinch me so I know I'm not dreaming.' She turned to Broderick.

'It's all real.' He gave a slow smile; evidently he understood her euphoria. 'It never ceases to inspire and delight me either.' He sat down on the grass and watched the last of the sun going down, throwing a russet haze over the sea.

This was too good an opportunity to miss. Serena snapped the most gorgeous sunset she'd ever witnessed in her life, and managed to get a picture of the gigantic bird that appeared overhead out of nowhere, as if wanting to be in on the shot.

'It's like being in the land of the dinosaurs,' she breathed.

She took more pictures and wondered for a moment whether to take one of Broderick himself, but thought better of it. There were enough palm tree and island silhouettes to be going on with.

The Wi-Fi was non-existent, but she scribbled furiously in her notebook while there was still enough light to see. Once the sun had begun to sink into the horizon, she didn't realise just how quickly the darkness would set in.

'I'll leave you with that, while I go and see to these, then.' He stood, picked up the bowl and turned back when she shouted after him.

'I really would like to do those dishes for you. It's only fair, seeing as you cooked the best fish supper I've ever eaten.'

'Wouldn't hear of it,' he shouted, as he disappeared down the other side of the bank. 'There's water down here if you need any for washing or to freshen up, anything like that.'

Quickly closing her notebook, she knew there would be time to catch up with her jottings in the morning, when she would be back on the island of Neptune. For now, she wanted to know where Broderick did the washing up.

She followed in the direction he'd gone, slowly until her eyes adjusted to the gloom. She could hear the sound of crashing water — that had to be where he was headed. She cast one last, longing look towards the ocean — she'd be lucky if she saw such a spectacular sight again in her life.

With holdall and camera draped across her shoulder, Serena tripped daintily down the grassy bank. She heard whistling; Broderick was engrossed in swilling the plates and cups.

'Ah, hello, it's the roving reporter, hot from the city desk,' he joked and put his hand to his ear, mimicking taking a phone call. 'Yes, I have a scoop, hold the front page.' He ducked to avoid the mock back-hander that Serena sent his way.

'Just because you know all there is to know about life on a desert island, Mr Broderick Loveday.' She couldn't help but laugh as she picked up the tea towel to dry the crocks. 'You're so good at these survival skills. Ever thought about running survival expeditions — you know, like Bear Grylls?' She shrugged when she saw the horror on his face. 'Only a thought — it would give you some income.'

'You can keep any more of those thoughts to yourself, little lady. Have you ever thought of going to New York and making a name for yourself taking photos of the Hudson River and all who sail on her, dead or alive, rather than being in paradise with me?'

Now he was coming over all grumpy again — and after such a delightful evening.

'Look, I didn't mean to tell you what to do. And that's a silly idea I had just now. Please ignore it.'

'I will. It's gone completely out of my head.' He collected the clean plates and cups, stacked them neatly in the bowl then picked it up. 'Now, are you fit to walk back to base? I happen to

116

know of a speciality coffee waiting to be sampled.'

He smiled, but his smoky-grey eyes were more guarded than they'd been earlier.

★ ★ ★

As she might have guessed, the coffee was mellow, and as rich as Broderick's tan was now after being back on his island for a few days.

'It's going to be a long night, seeing as I've got nowhere to sleep,' she mused. 'Maybe I'll just snuggle into the ground sheet and pull my cardigan over the top of me. Hope the midges aren't biting too much.'

She looked into the darkening sky. The buzz and clicking of crickets and other critters was really beginning to get going now, sounding as if they were in competition with each other to see who could croak, click and buzz the loudest.

'Try the hammock; it's always been

comfortable enough for me.' He pointed to the low slung bed.

For a moment, Serena hesitated.

'But it's your bed . . . ' Surely he didn't mean . . . ?

'Tonight it's yours. I'm sure it's clean, and if you like I'll spray some Midge-Away in there. Also there's a piece of netting to drape over your face. They'll seek out a new human right away.'

Serena gave a shudder.

'You make them sound like vampires. And I'm not used to getting into a hammock, how do you do it?' She held on to the side of the canvas, and decided she would keep all her clothes on. If there were flesh-eating and blood-sucking flying things going around, she would cover up completely.

'Watch me.' Broderick let her move out of the way, and then took hold of the edge of his bed and did a twirl. Instantly he was lying down in front of her, smirking back at her with his arms folded behind his head. 'What was difficult about that?' He relaxed for a moment, then swung out as quickly as he'd gone in. 'Now you try.'

In her mind, Serena gave a sigh and raised her eyes to the sky. She took a breath to steady herself, and focused on the robust canvas. It couldn't be that difficult, from the way he'd glided in. Holding the edge, she hauled herself into the swinging bed — and rolled straight out onto the ground on the other side.

She landed with a bump on soft grass so she wasn't hurt, apart from her pride.

Broderick was belly-laughing as if he were in a 'how hard and long can you laugh' contest.

'Ho ho, that was fantastic, best acrobatics I've seen for ages. Can I help you up?'

'No — thank you all the same, I can manage quite well by myself.'

Serena knew she must have made an ungainly sight, but he might have toned down the laughter to save her modesty.

The way he was going on, he'd wake all the vampire bats in the caves along the hillside. As it was, she was on the lookout for night mosquitoes, flying crickets, rats and wolves. Not that she was scared or anything — just a little wary and alert to dangers.

'It does feel a bit odd without a roof over my head. Surely you don't sleep in the open all the time like this, do you?'

It was one thing loving the great outdoors, and a night on the beach would be romantic with the right person — but in the middle of the trees, it was pretty dark and shadows danced around her.

'Well I know of a hut called Ackee Lodge, or something.' Broderick held his hands up as Serena threw him a look of disgust.

'You'll be quite safe, and if it helps, I'll be close by, over here.' He pointed to a ground sheet and a spare pillow. 'There is a barn where I go if it's the rainy season, but this is calm, and don't worry about the critters; we might have been teasing a little.' He gave her hand a reassuring squeeze.

Serena was glad of his warm touch, and without thinking, she reached up and gave him a hug, burying her head into his shoulder, as she might do with a good friend. She hadn't known him long, but she knew he would keep her safe. Suddenly embarrassed, she let him go.

'Sorry, I just wanted to say thanks for letting me use the bed. And I'll get back over to Neptune with the ferryman tomorrow.' She gave an uncertain smile. 'Unless . . . shall we try the barn?'

'Er, no, a nest of rats have taken up residence. It needs cleaning out first. And there's a hole in the roof . . . and the door is hanging off.'

Serena's heart plummeted.

'Right, then, I'll have another go at this.' She swallowed hard and leaned alongside the edge of the canvas bed. 'Here I jolly well go and . . . YES!'

She plunged into the soft canvas and it swung from side to side like a baby's cradle. Above her, she saw the stars beginning to twinkle and she wanted to laugh out loud.

'I did it. So go and laugh at yourself, Broderick Robinson Crusoe Loveday . . . '

She giggled to herself as she closed her eyes and she heard him chuckling not too far away.

7

The following morning, Serena roused and tried to work out where she was, and why she'd slept in a swinging bunk rather than a comfortable bed, and then she heard a rustle of leaves.

Of course, that was it! She peeped over the side of the hammock, hardly daring to breathe as she didn't want to attract attention. She listened and wondered what predator lay in the bushes. The open-air bed had been surprisingly comfortable and much better than sleeping on the ground, so she wouldn't complain.

She familiarised herself with the jungle-like surroundings. Broderick was busying himself with what she supposed were his usual morning tasks. Blinking sleep from her eyes, Serena wondered how it was she'd let him talk her into staying over in the wild outdoors in preference to being comfortably ensconced in that extra-large bed in Ackee Grove. *I must be mad*.

She watched him pour water from one container into another, and put a kettle on the fire. It looked as if he might be about to brew a cup of tea. That meant she must get up, because the thought of tea in a hammock was out of the question.

Just then, an almighty roar emanated from the thicket behind her.

The creature making the noise pounced — was it a crazy panther, or some other wild creature of the island? It made an unfamiliar sound, like nothing Serena had heard before.

She watched in horror as the attacker — it was a man, she could see now — leaped onto Broderick from behind and wrestled him to the ground. There was a scuffle and lots of grunting sounds. She hadn't a clue what to do.

She screamed out, 'What's happening? Broderick, can I help?'

Her words fell on deaf ears, so she grabbed the nearest item to hand, which happened to be a tin plate.

The kerfuffle continued, and the bundle of scrambled limbs blurred into one. Serena took aim and when Broderick rolled away from his attacker, she took her chance.

The wallop made a loud clanging sound, and at the same second she clipped the intruder, she heard Broderick shout, 'Don't use that! You might hurt Agwe.'

The clang would have been heard a mile away. His warning came too late. Serena gasped.

'Hurt Agwe? Oh no! I thought I was saving your life from one of the pirates. I thought he was going to kill you!'

She turned and her heart skipped a beat as she saw Agwe lying still.

'I really wish you wouldn't have done that. It's our self-defence programme.' Broderick glared at her. 'He surprises me whenever he thinks I might be off-guard, keeps me on my toes.' He knelt by his friend to check he was all right.

'Think yourself lucky you're not in a coma.' Broderick grinned at Agwe, who was now rubbing his head and attempting to sit up. 'Here, pal, try this.' He placed a flannel soaked in water across his friend's forehead, and then checked the bump that by now was beginning to resemble a golf ball on his head.

Serena glanced from one to the other.

'This is how you carry on your friendship? One of you might have got badly hurt. And all that noise — you must have woken all the wild animals around here for miles. Or should I rephrase that and say, you're both like a pair of wild animals! Why did you do that? I mean, is it a regular thing, or what?' Serena looked puzzled.

'It's how we make sure we're both ready for real intruders,' Agwe explained through a slight daze. 'We creep up and surprise each other when it's least expected. I thought with you here, he might be distracted and not ready in case of attack. Those are the times when it is good to check he's alert, and proves we're real friends.'

'Oh — I see.' Serena made a face. 'Do you expect attacks to occur regularly then?' She gave a shudder and reached for her jacket. Looking at Broderick, she thought he must have left behind some awful situation to be living in the wild, and having his best mate creep up on him when he was happily preparing breakfast.

Speaking of which, she was starving.

'That cuppa looks good,' she said, seeing tea was brewing. 'And what do you eat for breakfast?'

Serena could have wolfed down a bacon sandwich, but now she also looked forward to tropical fruits. She'd already seen chopped coconut on the side.

'How does eggs and spinach sound?' Broderick hauled Agwe to his feet in one swift move. His friend smiled his thanks.

'I'll get the children to bring eggs later if you need more. Have you enough for breakfast?'

Broderick nodded and showed him the few eggs he had in a basket.

Serena found it strange that someone who had been rolling on the floor wrestling like a crazy beast was now checking to see if they wanted more eggs. There was so much to learn about life on this tropical island, and so many questions she wanted to ask as well. Things like the rumour she'd heard about him falling from a cruise ship and getting stranded on the island . . .

'Now I need to go and help at home for a while. And, Brodders, please bring the lady over to meet the family later, before she goes back across the water.' The native waved and walked steadily inland, leaving Serena and Broderick alone.

The spinach omelette was utterly delicious; whatever herbs he'd used to enhance the flavour worked well. When he told her about the chives and wild parsley, garlic and thyme, Serena reached for her notebook.

'And there was spinach in there as well?'

'Surely you'd remember that? You don't need to write it down.'

She frowned. 'Of course I do. I'm a reporter, and I have to send articles back to the magazine I work for. They'd like some island recipes, and that omelette is the best I've ever eaten. Now, how did you cook the spinach — boiled or fried?'

* * *

The morning flew by. As they walked, Broderick pointed out all the wild flowers and trees, naming them and telling her the culinary or medicinal use of each one.

'This one, the Banyan tree, is used in herbal medicine.' Broderick took a sideways look at Serena. 'It's a fig tree.'

'You've studied the subject, then?' Now she was curious. 'Don't tell me you're a consultant who's got tired of NHS cuts and escaped out here?'

Stop gabbling and let the man speak. Serena, first rule of interviews, you have two ears and one mouth. LISTEN!

She reached out and touched the long tree trunks that looked like legs.

'Nothing of the sort. It's good for lowering cholesterol, and an anti-inflammatory. Agwe's wife will tell you more about the healing remedies if you ask her when we go over there later.' He made his way through the trees and headed towards the water supply. 'We'll top up the bottles while we're here.' He handed the smaller of the two canisters he was carrying to Serena.

'Didn't they try and rescue you — when you fell from the cruise ship, I mean?'

Serena pulled her forehead into a frown as she pictured him hurtling overboard from a huge liner. She flicked her long braids, decorated with multi-coloured bands, over her shoulder out of her way. 'Surely they have life-jackets and small boats for when folk fall overboard?'

'It was dark. Everyone was somewhere else. There was only me, out on deck, looking at the stars and wishing I was somewhere other than on board this huge sailing hotel. Everything was organised, and duly laid on, like entertainment, cinemas, all the food you can eat — yet it was like being in prison. I had to escape.'

For a moment he gazed at the gushing waterfall on the other side of the expanse of turquoise water. It culminated in a freshwater lagoon, like a private swimming pool. All this was fed by a river that had travelled down from higher land.

His mind had seemingly wandered to another place — and from the look of it, that place wasn't somewhere he felt comfortable with.

Serena had frozen.

'You jumped! It was no accident, was it? You wanted to escape so badly . . . Oh my Lord, who were you with at the time, and do they know where you are now? Please tell me you've let them know — and how about your parents? Was that where you'd been when you were in London?'

She was gabbling again, she couldn't help herself. He was less a castaway than a runaway!

The splash as he dived into the water soaked her and she screamed.

'You can't keep running away. Who did you visit in England?' Serena examined her soaked cut-offs and T-shirt. 'Ugh, I've only got the clothes I came over in. These need washing already.'

'Well, come on in, then. It's the easiest and quickest way to wash your entire outfit.'

He reached out and she gasped as he pulled her into the crystal-fresh water. She wondered if he was slightly crazy. In fact, no — he was the most eccentric man she'd ever met, but the way he'd wrestled with his mate earlier showed sharp reactions and survival skills. The bushy beard, now flattened to his jaw, made him look older than his years. She wondered about his age, but did not dare ask more questions for now. This trip was turning out to be a revelation.

He flipped over and dived. The water felt cool and refreshing on her skin. She always did love to dive in the swimming baths, just as he'd done then. With a quick twist, head down, she took a dive under the water and almost landed on top of him, then pushed herself back up for air.

'I'm sorry, didn't mean to land in the same place as you.' Floundering for a moment, she trod water until she got her balance. 'Oh, it's lovely and cool.'

Serena held her face to the golden rays that shone through the lush trees. She turned and looked at him, surprised to see him watching her.

'This is the way you do your washing, then?'

'Of course not — only with a lady present, it wouldn't do to get the clobber off, would it now? I'll come back later when you've gone.'

'Well, don't let me stop you getting on with your routine. I'm sure Agwe and Daniel will be ready before long.' She flicked water at his face as he shook water from his hair.

'Would you like to meet his family? You saw some of the children when you arrived, I'm sure they'd like to meet you. His wife is really friendly. I don't intrude much, but I'll never hear the last of it if I don't take you to see them.'

He scrambled from the water and reached for one of the two towels he'd hung on a tree nearby. 'We can leave the water in the containers just here in the hollow. It'll be safe until I get back.'

Glancing up towards the rising sun, he leaned forward and dried his face, neck and head, then threw Serena the other towel. 'Here, just give yourself a rub over, you'll soon dry off.'

'Thanks.' It occurred to Serena that she could easily stay on the island and enjoy the fun and easy company of her new friend. Work had definitely been placed on a back burner in her mind — but that was her reason for being here, so she must focus on that. For now, though, she really looked forward to meeting Agwe's family.

* * *

'Just about another half a mile and we'll be there.'

Serena wished she could have changed into a summer dress and a pair of trendy sandals. At least her hair felt tidy with the braids.

'Do I look presentable?' She dusted herself down and stood up straight. Somehow she knew he'd tell her the truth, whatever that may be. He wasn't a man to hold back on his opinions.

'You look a proper Jungle Jane — these are the ideal thing for out here.' He gave a gentle tug on her hair. 'Stop worrying, it's not like back home. Nobody will give a fig what you're wearing. Come on, only a bit further and we'll be there.'

The pathway widened into a dusty road, and they could hear the squeals of children at play. Tall crops grew either side of the road, and Broderick told her it was sugar cane.

'You've heard Agwe talk about the rum smuggling? This is where it all began — only don't tell him I told you that.' He winked. Now Serena had a whole load of new questions to ask.

The children were the first to greet them, and they ran to Broderick as if he were an uncle, jumping around him and looking shyly at Serena.

'It's Brodders, and he's got a lady with him — the one who came on the boat!' The screams of excitement almost made Serena feel like royalty. She'd never been introduced to someone in that way before and if she had any nerves or misgivings at all on meeting Agwe's family, they were dissolved in an instant. She couldn't help the giggles that bubbled up inside her.

'Are they always like this?' She

136

turned and grinned at Broderick.

'Absolutely not; they wouldn't look twice at me normally — but then again, I do sometimes have to creep up quietly and make sure Agwe is on the lookout for muggers or wild bears.'

Serena opened her eyes in surprise. 'Really, are there? You never said to me . . . '

Broderick doubled up laughing. 'You were the one saying Bear Grylls might be around here somewhere. Perhaps you're disappointed that you've not found an explorer, or a wild bear.' He lifted his shoulders and gave a nonchalant grin. 'You'll make your boyfriend back home jealous.'

She shook her head in exasperation at his games and teasing, which came as a surprise. He had more layers to his personality than anyone she'd ever met. From Mr Grumps to the romantic bard by the camp-fire, to the joker when he came in contact with the family who were his closest neighbours — then sometimes he was sullen and had a dark side. If only he could talk to her, maybe she could help . . .

The clearing gave way to reveal a circle of barn-like buildings. A handful of goats were wandering apparently freely, but then Serena noticed a tether dragging with them. Agwe and Daniel sat at a table with benches attached.

'Ah, welcome. We were wondering if you'd come and join us, or be busy talking plans.'

'Talking plans?' Serena looked at Brodders.

'I told them you're on a mission, and we're happy to help with your research.'

At that moment Agwe's wife appeared. She wore a bright floral dress and she was very pretty, with dark hair, olive skin and the most expressive eyes that offered a warm welcome.

'Come on — I made treats. We were expecting you before now. What kept you?'

She was joking, Serena could tell from the warm and friendly smile being directed her way.

'We had some washing to do.'

She couldn't stop a smile from breaking out across her lips as she recalled their antics earlier.

8

'Cindy has made us a drink with freshly squeezed limes — some I picked early this morning — and pineapple and ginger mint to flavour it.'

The love Agwe felt for his wife was clear from the way he watched her every move, then proudly poured a glass of her concoction each for Serena and Broderick, making sure everyone else gathered there had plenty as well.

'That would be after your combat moves over in Camp Broderick, you mean? Sorry about the collateral damage.'

Serena knew he hadn't had limes with him then, so obviously he'd found a tree on his way back. Serena tasted the drink and immediately felt refreshed. The sprigs of light and dark green leaves used to decorate the drink, along with rings of fresh lime, added a special touch.

Cindy emerged from her home to join them, carrying a plate of interesting-looking biscuits.

'I'd really like to know how the lime drink is made, if you don't mind sharing your secrets.' Serena took another drink and immediately the tang of limes hit the back of her throat.

'It's so easy to do.' Cindy smiled and pulled up a chair near Serena. 'Chop lots of limes, and then add them to a pan of water. Bring to the boil and simmer on the hob. Add to that some beautiful demerara sugar made on the island — oh, and a vanilla pod.' Cindy ticked off on her fingers all the ingredients of her home-made squash. 'Or if you haven't one of those, some spices like half a cup of chopped ginger.'

Cindy looked around proudly, indicating any glass that wasn't full to Agwe, who made sure to keep everyone's drink topped up.

'Even though it's made with limes, we still call it lemonade — or better known as lime-water or swank. This is us having our swanky drink, you see. Or on a weekday we call it wash.' Cindy's laughter rang out across the clearing, and some of the children ran to her side. One little boy climbed up onto her lap. 'Now, who is going to taste the coconut cookies for Mammy and let me know if they taste alright for the lady visitor?'

A chorus of, 'Me, me,' echoed around as they politely formed a queue and gently lifted one each from the plate.

'Your children are really sweet and so well-behaved. How many have you got altogether?' Two girls and two boys were at the table, but other children were clustering round. And there was a small crowd the first day she arrived. Surely they couldn't all be hers?

'Come on, don't be shy, the lady is asking about you,' Cindy called to two little girls who were holding hands. 'Now, these little darlings are our nieces. Uncle Agwe is going to teach you both to fish soon, isn't he?'

Nodding heads in unison and then treating Serena to their widest gap-toothed smiles, the sisters reached for a biscuit when Cindy offered them the plate.

'Oh, where are my manners! Would you like to try one, Serena? Now, you were asking about our children. Come and say hello, everyone.'

Cindy clapped her hands and a girl who looked the image of her leaned out of a window.

'What's up, Mammy? I'm going over to Neptune with Shami and Rhawand in a bit. I've got time to make more biscuits if that's what you want.'

'Did you ask your daddy if it's all right? You know how he feels about those two.'

The window banged shut and the girl sloped sulkily outside.

'If you must know, they're taking me across for free and Xanthe is coming with me, so they'll be more interested in talking to her, seeing as she's got all that long blonde hair.' The girl looked at Serena and studied her braided hair.

'Your hair is pretty — just like your mother's,' she told the girl, smiling. Drat — probably not the best thing to say to a rebellious teenager.

'This is Sky-Blou, our eldest.'

Agwe overheard the conversation and chimed in, 'She's growing more beautiful by the day, and you be careful. Stick together, you and Xanthe. Any trouble from those Buccaneers and they'll find themselves walking the plank. Tell them that from me.'

One by one, Serena was introduced to the family of Agwe and Cindy — six children altogether.

'Come on, all of you. This is Blossom.' A girl with olive skin and long dark plaits smiled shyly. Either side of her, holding her hands, were two identical boys. 'The twins are named Forrest and River, and they're always playing games to trick me, aren't you?' Cindy scolded, but Serena could see she was only having fun. The boys looked a mixture of both their parents. Cindy pointed.

'That's Sidney; you might guess he'd be with Broderick. They talk about poetry and English literature if ever they get the chance.' She shouted the boy over and he politely shook hands, before returning to his seat. 'Now, if you happen to be walking in the shrubbery and a small boy jumps out at you, even painted up in disguise, that will be Arrow. He's been taking lessons from his dad and watching him and Broderick grappling, so there's no hope for that one turning out well, is there?'

Cindy's loving tone belied her words. She was obviously smitten with all her children.

Now Sky-Blou was waving goodbye, dressed in colourful shorts and a white blouse tied in a knot at her waist.

Serena imagined the Buccaneers must be less threatening than she first thought if Agwe and Cindy allowed their daughter to take a trip across to Neptune with them. Then again, she was going with her friend.

Now Serena really wanted to sample Cindy's cooking, and she soon convinced herself the swim and walk had burned off most of the calories from the breakfast Broderick had made earlier. She looked to the plate in front of her and her eyes widened.

'I can't say no — they look delicious and I see the children are back for more, which means they must be yummy.'

She took a delicate bite from a biscuit that had a drizzle of white icing on top, and closed her eyes tasting the freshness of the juicy, shredded coconut and a hint of something more fruity like mango or peach.

Will anyone back home miss me if I just stay here forever? That was the effect the cookie had on her. Thoughts of home jogged her memory. She wondered if her mum and dad had the Christmas tree up yet. *I really must phone home when I get back on the Island of Neptune.*

Serena looked at Cindy and could only shake her head in wonderment.

'You're a lady of many talents, and I think you've got your hands full with looking after everyone.' Serena took her chance to ask Cindy how she felt about the ambush games that took place between her husband and Broderick. 'I do understand they're keeping in practice, but you must worry about them getting hurt.'

'They're big boys now, and I think they do quite well looking after themselves.' Cindy smiled knowingly in Serena's direction, then looked to where Broderick was chatting but sneaking a glance towards them now and then. 'You like him a lot, don't you?'

'Don't be silly-I hardly know the man.' Serena felt herself blushing. 'Well — he's all right when he's in a good mood, like now.'

At that moment Broderick gave his belly laugh and caused them both to laugh along with him.

'My husband always has a fully stocked medical cabinet, on the offchance he might get hurt. That doesn't happen often, though.'

She looked Serena square in the eye and the reporter winced.

'I'm awfully sorry — only I thought Broderick was being attacked for real early this morning. I did something to halt him in his tracks and I can't apologise enough, really I can't.'

She looked across to where Broderick spoke easily, then laughed and joked with Agwe and Daniel. Gone was the grumpy stranger. Here among friends he was happy, she could see that.

As if sensing her watching him, he looked up, and raised an eyebrow in her direction. He mouthed, 'Five,' and lifted his hand, indicating that they might be ready to get on their way soon.

She watched him stand up and say his goodbyes to the children and his mates. Next minute, he was by her side.

'Listen — ' He leaned in to whisper.

'I'm not brilliant at goodbyes, so maybe we'll meet up, sometime soon. It's been, mmm, you know . . . '

She found it strange how someone who could recite poetry with such feeling by the camp fire, was suddenly unable to say anything coherent. Then again, she was unsure what to say either.

He turned and waved to the others as he disappeared into the trees.

Serena struggled to hide her disappointment at the emptiness he'd left behind, but taking stock of the situation, she shook herself and smiled at the family. She'd wanted to tell Broderick how much she'd enjoyed the stay, the breakfast, the fun, and ask whether he would mind if she came again. And was he married?

Then she brought her attention back to the people who had shown her so much kindness and hospitality in a short space of time.

'It's been a pleasure to meet you and all the family. Is it your sister who lives nearby, or your brother?'

Cindy looked puzzled for a moment, and then understood. 'Ah, because of all our nieces and nephews around, you mean? Actually, both my brother and sister live a short walk over a hill. Paul with his wife, she's expecting another, and Sapphire with her husband. We're a really close family; our father lives a little further along in a home-made village, entirely his own, he's a herbalist. Sadly my mother died too young, but I really don't want to talk about that. My dad taught me all I know about herbs.'

Agwe walked over and caught the tail end of the conversation. 'What this lady does not know about herbs and healing isn't worth knowing.' He wrapped his arms around his wife and leaned in to place a kiss on the end of her nose.

'I really could sit and talk to you all day.' Serena looked towards Daniel. 'Are you waiting to go? I don't want to hold you up if you're ready.'

'There are a few of us. Agwe, his

brother-in-law and one of the nephews will accompany us on the way back, so there will be another boat as well. No hurry — only we need to be gone sometime within the next hour, or so.'

Yes! She might have time, if she left now, to catch up with Broderick so she could say goodbye properly. To heck with all his *I don't like to say goodbye* rubbish.

'Well, thank you for the lovely refreshments. Actually, just remembered, I've left my lens cap for the camera back at Camp Broderick — where do we sail from?'

She felt an awful fraud, but they weren't in any immediate hurry to leave . . . and she did want to double check there was nothing of hers lying around near where she'd slept.

'You know where we landed, among the trees that draped into the sea, and a bit further along, there was a great big wide sandy beach, full of shells?' Daniel spoke with precision as if she might have forgotten the momentous landing.

'Of course. That's where I need to meet you?'

He nodded. 'Any time in the afternoon, we'll catch fish if we're waiting.'

Gathering her things, Serena looked around gratefully at everyone.

'Thank you for being so friendly and kind. I really would love to see you again. Hopefully, I'll be back.'

After lopsided smiles from some of the boys, a polite handshake from Blossom then even a biscuity kiss from the youngest, Serena headed off, back along the track to base camp.

She scrambled over tree roots and jumped ditches, following the pathway and enjoying the birdsong and screeches of the animals scurrying up the trees as she approached. It felt much quicker going back than on the way coming, and she soon came to the clearing where the hammock and camp fire smouldered.

No sign of Broderick. She looked to see if the water carrier was by the kitchen area; it wasn't.

There was only one place he would have gone; to gather more water, have a wash, or swim even.

She scrambled up the hill, avoiding looking at at the view in case she missed the chance to snatch a few more minutes with her friend. Even though he'd probably be mad at her for bothering, she tottered steadily down the rambling pathway.

The sound of the gushing waterfall was the first thing she heard, then the screech of a parrot or a cockatoo. The heat was overwhelming. She crouched down to peer through the trees to see if there was any sign of Broderick by the lagoon.

And then she spotted the island man, standing naked under the tumbling crescendo of water, eyes closed and his face upturned into the spray. He twirled around, keeping his feet steady on the rocks, only stopping to reach for a bottle of shower gel on the ledge which he massaged into his hair, then his beard. The lather sent a riot of soapy bubbles tumbling down his hairy chest and onto his firm . . . and lithe . . . and tanned . . . and . . . just wow . . . the fittest male body she'd ever seen naked before.

Serena sat down and couldn't help but stare. He hadn't seen her; she could just disappear, not say a word and remember the vision. The back view of Brodders as he turned in a circle under his outdoor shower wasn't half bad either. How did he have such a pert behind? He surely resembled a centrefold in Playgirl magazine, if there was such a thing. She didn't know — but what she did know was that it was going to be awfully hard to tear herself away from here for a while yet. He looked good enough to eat.

As she stood up, she couldn't think why her legs were trembling and she could hardly walk. Gingerly she stepped nearer. When she trod on a twig, it snapped loudly and he heard the noise over the thundering of the falls. He

154

shook his head and cleared his face of soap suds.

'Who's there? Agwe, if that's you, I'm in no mood for combat moves. Leave it, and if it's not Agwe, go away — whoever you are.' He reached for a towel that was on the bank nearby.

'It's me again.' *Oh! What's happened to my voice, it's gone all squeaky and I'm talking like one of the Bee Gees.* 'Er, just came to say one last goodbye, you needn't have rushed off — they aren't sailing for a while yet.'

It was all Serena could do to stop staring at him. She had to force herself to look away while he stepped into his underpants and shorts. Even when he'd pulled his shirt on, and the light jungle jacket that he always wore, she couldn't see him as the same man any more.

How had she missed that beautiful body? She must be going blind. He was a master of disguise — the beard covered his face so much that she'd accepted he was the lonely eccentric he appeared from the poetry he loved reading by the camp fire.

'You make a habit of creeping up on a man having a shower, do you?' His words sounded harsh, but the hint of a smile played around his lips. 'If I'd known you were going to follow me, I'd have brought a towel for you as well.'

Glad that he broke the silence, Serena hoped her voice would be normal next time she spoke. Swallowing hard, she looked at his face.

'You're a bit of a mystery to me. How come — seriously, I'm leaving soon so you can tell me honestly — why are you here?' She found her eyes wandering to his tanned legs and the curly black hair that covered his shins. 'Are you married and you've done that jumping overboard trick — then did you take a flight to London to see if your wife is missing you?' Serena tapped her fingers on her lips. 'Let me see, she decided she'll get on fine without you and it's made you grumpy because you still love her and wish you'd never jumped?'

'Wrong on all counts, apart from the

jumping overboard — I'll admit to that.' He ran a hand through his grey-streaked dark curls, then looked at her and smiled. 'Do you believe in fate?'

His question knocked her off her flow, and when his dark grey eyes looked deep into her own, she felt as if she'd just gone round the loop-the-loop on the Big Dipper at Brighton beach.

'I think I do — yes.'

She had to. How else, as a junior reporter on a magazine, not long in the job, would she be sitting on a Caribbean island with a delicious hunk only inches away from her . . . and all the time in the world to get up to anything they liked?

Darn! That jelly legs feeling was back again.

'I really came back to check I hadn't left my lens cap or anything else important under the hammock.' Serena attempted to stand up, but her legs gave way. Broderick held out his large hand out and hauled her up.

'And here was me thinking you'd

come back because you were missing me already. With you it's all about the photos, the story, the article, and the newspapers.' A frown creased his brow.

They began walking back to where the boat would be waiting. Instinctively grasping his hand as she stumbled back over the uneven pathway, Serena looked out to sea, and whispered to herself, 'And there was me, thinking I'd never see such a sight as that . . . little did I know.'

She smiled up at Broderick, who appeared to be studying her face. Then he pulled her gently to sit on the ground with him.

'They're only down there — it's OK, they'll be fishing for a while yet. They're never in a hurry to leave here — any more than I am.'

Taking her hand, he gently stroked her fingers.

'Stay . . . just one more night. I didn't have chance to walk with you on the beach and show you the stars — how low and bright they can be this time of the year.'

'But Agwe and Daniel . . . ? They'll wonder what's going on, and I know you don't like goodbyes, but . . . '

'I know — the articles have to be sent and the drunken monkeys need to be found. How about if you stay one more night, and I'll ask Agwe to leave out the dramatics, and I really will give you plenty of detail on where to find them — the monkeys, I mean. Do we have a deal?'

'Well — the deal is, if I stay tonight — providing that's all right with Agwe and Daniel — then no sneaking off. I'll expect you to stand on the sand and wave me off. Just like in the films.'

She smiled and reached up for a friendly hug — only now she found it hard to think of him as a friend. It would be even harder to say goodbye to this incredible man she'd only just met. He smelled enticingly of pine and sandalwood.

'It's a deal,' he whispered.

The touch of his lips so close to her

ear gave her a fuzzy feeling and she couldn't help wondering whether his hammock was suitable for two. Apart from that, she really didn't want to put him out of his own bed for a second night in a row . . .

The thoughts drifting through her mind gave her cause to blush, and she hoped she would be able to control herself. She really wasn't that kind of girl . . . but maybe that Caribbean swank drink had gone to her head.

Either that, or life on the island was having a strange effect on her.

9

There's something I want to do for you.' Broderick looked at Serena; he'd gone all serious again.

'What's that?' She hardly dare ask . . . share a shower with her, maybe?

'It's the bed; it's more of a nap sack than a bedtime bed. I'll build something in the trees — it'll be more comfortable and you'll be guaranteed a good night's sleep.'

Serena didn't know whether to laugh, say thank you or cry into her handkerchief.

'That sounds good,' was the best answer she could come up with.

'Let's go and find the crew. They won't mind leaving the trip over to Neptune until tomorrow, though I know Agwe likes to keep an eye on that daughter of his when she's off with the bad boys.' He smiled. 'Only they're just kids, being kids and having fun.'

Looking straight ahead, he began to lead the way to the spot where Serena had arranged to meet up, ready to catch the lift over the water.

Now she'd seen him with his clothes off, she felt she could talk more freely.

'What did you do for fun when you were younger?' Half expecting him to say *mind your own business*, she lifted a stray branch from a raspberry bramble to avoid prickling her legs, then strode forward to walk beside him.

'Usual things most boys do, I suppose. Riding a bike was one of my first pleasures. Lego, Meccano — what about you? Don't tell me, let me guess . . . A Post Office set and a microscope. Or was it one of those portable typewriters? My sister had one, that's how I know.'

'Actually, yes, I did have a typewriter and lots of notebooks of course. Not that I'm saying it wasn't fun but I meant outdoorsy stuff, like climbing trees. I remember a great rope swing we used to play on, all of us kids from where we lived. We'd dare each other and see who'd be able to swing clear across the brook, and who would fall in.'

'Ah, yes, life isn't worth living unless you've got a rope swing, is it? There's one rigged up further along the ravine, I'll show you later. Here we are — as I thought, engrossed in what they're doing.' Broderick held the larger branches to one side, making room for Serena to follow him.

They walked onto the beach and watched as Agwe and Daniel instructed the twins, River and Forrest, on how to land their catch that was trying its best to escape the line. They fished from the small jetty where a couple of colourful boats secured nearby bobbed in the light breeze.

'Serena's staying one more night; we didn't have much time to chat about things.'

Agwe was the first to laugh and throw a comment their way. 'Chat about things, yes, that's a good name for it.' His white teeth gleamed against his brown skin and he wasn't at all perturbed.

Broderick stopped him in his tracks. 'Look, seriously, Agwe . . . can we forget about the ambush moves tonight? Come round, but I'm going to get cracking with making a tree bed for the lady, and I'll be in the hammock — or I might make a couple of tree house bunks.' He threw a quick glance in Serena's direction, and then spoke to the others.

'We'll have a massive pot of jambal-aya; you're all invited, of course. Bring Cindy and the kids. Then she can check she taught me how to cook it properly.' Broderick turned to Serena. 'It'll be a chance for you to hear Agwe's family singing, reciting poetry — they're a joy, and so talented.'

Serena's dream of a romantic night by the fire evaporated like the morning dew.

'It sounds like fun.' It was hard to

hide her disappointment, but what was she expecting? He'd been nothing but a gentleman, even if a bit of a moody one at first. Now he was planning an island get-together, with all of his friends. It would be a perfect way to end her mini-break on this small island. Secretly, though, she knew of a better one.

'Can I do something to help with the preparations?' She forced herself to be cheery and not sulk. He did like her a bit, she knew that, but he clearly didn't feel the same powerful spark she felt whenever she looked at him. Perhaps if she went and took a naked shower, he'd follow and . . .

Stop it, now, Serena Winter, behave!
'Just be there and keep me company.' He smiled and his grey eyes were full of warmth. 'I'd forgotten how it feels, to have another person close by to share things; someone to talk to and share the view of the sunset. It's the little things, don't you think?'

Her cheeks warmed slightly, but she

looked him in the eye.

'You have Agwe, his family, and the other island folk.' It sounded as if he was just glad of anyone to be there. The lonely island man wasn't such a loner after all.

Broderick shook his head. 'No — they all have each other. I walk alone — only a certain nosey journalist seems to have got herself attached and tangled up in my affairs.'

'Ah, now, speaking of affairs, what I wanted to know was . . . Arggghhhh!' Serena felt herself being scooped up into Broderick's strong arms and he held her tightly as he ran towards the shore. 'Put me down! I was only asking.'

Among the screams, she laughed and beat her fists against his chest, though she didn't really want to be released from his firm grasp.

'Are you going to stop asking questions?' He lowered her near to where gentle waves lapped the sand. 'Was that yes?' She almost touched the salty water. The day was hot and humid; it didn't bother her one bit when he placed her softly into the waves and sat down beside her in the shallows.

As if they'd been waiting in the trees and watching out for when it might be playtime, a gang of children appeared from nowhere. They ran squealing across the sand to join them, one by one they splashed into the water and began jumping and diving behaving like a shoal of little fishes. Serena had an overwhelming feeling of being among friends, and she was so glad he'd persuaded her to stay one more night.

'Can I show you where to get the best shells?' Blossom paddled through the waves and stood nearby, then gave a shy smile and politely asked Broderick, 'Is it all right if I show your friend?'

'Well, that sounds like a good idea, and I'm off to see what the lads have caught over there. I'm sure Serena would love to do that with you, Blossom. It's really kind of you to ask.'

He threw a cheeky smile in Serena's direction and then flicked a shower of brine over her with his toe from the shallow sea. She reciprocated, scooping a handful of ocean in his direction, which sailed past when he dived out of the way.

'Missed! You'll have to try better than that to catch me. Have fun searching for shells.'

He laughed and gave them both a wave as he strode off, his hair blowing in the breeze as he looked up to where a great cheer had erupted from the fishermen.

When she'd met him, his hair was charcoal-dark with grey strands around his ears and forehead. Now those grey bits had been bleached by the sun and along with the golden tan, he had the aura of a well-worn island dweller.

She watched him as he joined the others, and her heart flipped and started beating harder and faster. The fact that he wasn't interested in a quick grope, or any physical contact other than mucking around, made her fancy him and hunger for his touch all the more.

Blossom spoke quietly. 'We don't have to search — there are lots, and I have a little shed in the back garden. Well, it's my daddy's but I use it to practise making shell bracelets. Every single one is different, and one day I'd like to sell them on the market over there.' She pointed in the direction of the Island of Neptune. 'Broderick has been showing me how to thread them up and make pretty things. He's good at making things.'

Serena smiled and tilted her head. 'That's a great idea, Blossom. I think it's very enterprising of you. Have you told anyone your plans?'

The young girl looked down and played with her sarong style dress. She spoke quietly.

'Not really, it's only a dream, but I do go to the markets with Mammy when we have lots to sell. We always do well and I think the tourists would like my bracelets and necklaces.'

'How about you take me to see these lovely shells you were talking about? Do you know what they're called?'

* * *

Serena passed a pleasing couple of hours with the girl, who seemed destined to become a good little businesswoman. Blossom showed her a range of plain and multi-coloured shells ranging from pea-sized to shells the size of peaches, the largest being more like natural, beautiful ornaments that would grace any modern home. Blossom was right in thinking they'd make ideal gifts for holiday makers and travellers. She also had some made from peach stones and dried circles of lemons, limes and oranges.

Since meeting Cindy and her hus-band, and their charming family, on the Island of Shells — that's what Blossom told her it was called — Serena almost began to hope that she might have a family of her own, one day. It came as a surprise; she'd never even contemplated the idea until now.

Wondering if a little boy would resemble Broderick or a girl might take after her, she looked up when Blossom handed her more shells and a bag to put them in, made from an old fishing net.

'Do you love him?' The large eyes watched her, looking for a reaction and searching her face for clues. 'I know about things like love. Sky-Blou gets all weird when she goes out with Xanthe and the lads on the speedboat.' She threaded small shells onto some fishing twine and looked up.

'How does Sky-Blou get?' Serena trailed her hand through the sand, looking for more of the razor shells Blossom had asked for. 'What sort of thing do you mean?'

'All silly and acting like . . . you know . . . childish. How you and Brodders were in the sea earlier. It's all right, I won't tell tales. Just wondering, that's all.' She gave a little knowing smile, making her appear much older than she really was.

Giving a wide smile, Serena turned to her. 'Now then, Miss Blossom, I think you're a really clever girl, and you will make a brilliant jewellery maker.' Pushing a wayward lock of Blossom's thick hair back into her headband, Serena gave her hands a squeeze. 'But I think you'd make an even better detective or police officer, judging from the way you observe people.'

'Mammy tells me it's being nosey, but it's not. I'm only interested in people, and I'm learning about body language. Anyway, do you love him?'

'If you mean Broderick, and I presume you do?' Serena glanced at the young girl. 'Let's just say I like him quite a lot, as a friend. Now, come on, let's go and see how many fish they've caught, and we can show off with our shells.'

They carried the shells in the fish net bag and Serena wanted to laugh when she recalled their private little chat. She didn't realise her feelings showed, or that the friendship might be moving on a bit quicker than she intended. Maybe she'd tell Broderick later. Then looking into the smiling face of Blossom — who, she thought, would also make a good matchmaker — she decided that some things were best kept for girls' ears only and she smiled back.

★ ★ ★

Rhawand, at the wheel of the speed boat, asked the girls if they wanted him to go faster.

A chorus of 'Yes!' was bellowed out, followed by screams and laughter. Sky-Blou had known the terrible twosome for a long while and though they were known as the local bad boys, she and her friend were having fun.

'There's a map, showing where the treasure is.' Shami sat astride the bench in the speed boat as it tilted over the waves and looped around another of the small islands dotted around the Caribbean.

They all knew the dangers of the sea and Shami made sure that life-jackets were in the box of gear they kept under the seats of the boat. He had handed one each to the girls.

'Stick one of these over your head. I don't want an ear-bashing from your dad.' He looked at Sky-Blou and smiled. *'If anything happens to my little girl, you'll be under the sea quicker than a pirate's parachute.* That's what he told me last week when I dropped him some crates of beer off.' Shami gave an exaggerated shrug. 'As if we're stupid enough to let anything happen to you two. Anyway, I told him we're mates, just hanging out together, right?'

Sky-Blou nodded.

'Of course — and we wanted to get over to the market after going for a spin as well, didn't we, Xanthe?' Her friend agreed. 'What map were you talking about, and what kind of treasure?' Her eyes widened and she gave Xanthe a nudge.

Tapping the side of his nose, Shami whispered, 'There's a job coming up — or going down.' He gave a giggle. Both girls knew the lads were always trying to get in on deals and propositions that cropped up, but more often than not they came out smelling of bats' droppings — a saying her mammy was fond of using.

'We'll say it's going down.' Sky-Blou was impatient to hear what job, and what treasure was to be found. 'Tell us, then, before it's time for us to be dropped off in Neptune harbour.' She sat upright and glanced at the change of direction and how Rhawand was heading towards the larger island.

'It's your dad's Bonafide — that one who's got the bushy beard.' Shami always used the Caribbean slang for friend — Sky-Blou knew who he meant straight away.

'Well?' She made an exaggerated gesture.

'Let's say there's dollar to be made and me and him are the ones to proceed with Operation Treasure Map.' He spoke a bit more haughtily than normal and as the harbourside of Neptune was approaching, he took the jackets from the girls and put them back under the seat. 'And I trust this information will go no further, girls. Free travel will be waiting when you wish to return.'

Shami took the wheel and Rhawand sat back on the bench after they'd given Sky-Blou and Xanthe a helping hand to get out of the boat.

With a roar of the engine, Shami let rip with the boat and sped off to find more passengers who would pay good dollar to be ferried across the ocean. More often than not, they hunted for gossip and useful information that might be worth more than money. They were the Caribbean Buccaneers — they lived simply, and knew mostly everything there was to know around the islands.

'You shouldn't have told them,' Rhawand shouted to his mate, irritated by his loose lips. 'She'll tell her daddy and then they'll be on the alert.'

'No, she won't — why else would I have told her? If you trust me, then you'll realise she'll help lead us to the treasure. Now hang on tight and watch out . . .'

Shami pulled on the throttle, causing the boat to speed off at an alarming rate, giving Rhawand a drenching when he fell backwards off the seat and a great wave sprayed over the side of the boat. The Caribbean Buccaneers could be heard screeching with laughter as they sped along the Eastern side of the island of Neptune.

★ ★ ★

Meanwhile, in the Atlantis Hotel, Kathleen-Miranda Beckingsworth sipped on her gin and tonic with the map her wayward boyfriend had left behind in his man-drawer — or in truth, the map she had sneaked from there when he stormed off on his ramblings, tucked safely in her oversized Yves Saint Laurent handbag.

10

I don't feel guilty for keeping you here; you should be working, but I'm selfish, and you wanted to know more about life in the Caribbean, so let's compromise.'

Broderick took Serena's hand and smiled.

'How about if I show you some of the more interesting parts of the island — and then later on, I'll cook while you relax.' He pulled her towards him. 'You're fun to have around.' He laughed. 'That's when you're not crowning my friends over the head with breakfast plates or spiralling yourself over the edge of my hammock and landing in a heap on the grass.' Broderick stifled a laugh and gallantly offered his arm.

Serena forced her thoughts away from the beach, and linked her arm through his.

'Don't fret too much, you're hardly keeping me prisoner. I could have gone back over to Neptune, and maybe I should have, because the longer I stay here, it's as if . . . ' She didn't want to say it, but the Island of Shells was growing on her. And now that Agwe had taken the children back to the smallholding for a salad lunch with Daniel, she was all alone, with her own Robinson Crusoe.

'The island does get under your skin. It's how I felt after only a few days, when I landed here. That was over two years ago.'

He bent to pick up a pebble, running his thumb over the surface to reveal a turquoise blue tint with white marble effects running through it. Looking towards Serena, his eyes twinkled.

'Larimar . . . the stone of the lost city of Atlantis, that's another name for it, and every now and then gemstones get washed up. It's known as the healing stone, and any time the dolphins are near, it's said that a piece of this gem stone appears as well.'

'And you believe that?' She was astonished to think someone who'd been a master of finances, if what he said was true, could believe that dolphins and the stone of Atlantis were connected.

'A million pebbles on all the beaches in the whole world, and it can take a lifetime to find the right one.' He placed the aqua-blue stone into her hand, and then kicked at another pebble with his boot before picking it up and skimming it across the water. 'You can swim with dolphins just around the headland over there.'

He pointed to the tip of the island that curved round, showing a steep cliff pathway going up, or acres of silver sandy beaches to walk along.

Serena wished this time would last forever and clasped the gift in her palm before tucking it deep into the pocket of her shorts.

'Tell me about your family. I

promise I won't pry too much. You must have a girlfriend, or a wife back home.' She looked at him defiantly. 'I won't judge you or run away, only I'd like to know. And in case you were wondering, my last fling with a colleague from the office fizzled out before it got going, months ago. My job is my life.' She couldn't help a chuckle escaping her. 'Not that you'd think it right now — but usually it is.'

Serena turned away as they descended to where a sparkling sea invited them, knowing her words sounded trite. Here on the silken sandy beach, feeling soft sand scrunching between her toes as she walked at Broderick's side, how could she even think of work?

You'd better buck up your ideas soon, missus, otherwise you'll have no job to go back to . . .

One look at her walking companion and she didn't care a jot. It would be easy enough to catch up; she'd explain about the lack of Wi-Fi access.

Broderick was speaking. 'Relation-ships aren't something I feel comfortable talking about much. Other than to say, I haven't met the right person up to now. Perhaps I'm too much of an individualist to be with anyone.' He gave a half-smile. 'Not to worry. The right lady will cross my path when I least expect it. That's according to the Ju Ju man. If you believe a word he says.' He opened his eyes wide and gave a mock shiver.

'Who's the Ju Ju man? We used to have sweets called that when I was little.' Serena imagined Broderick was referring to some kind of fortune teller and it sounded as if the Ju Ju man had predicted a relationship for Broderick. How dare he suggest that Robinson Crusoe meet a lady — he seemed to be doing fine on his own! She decided to drop the relationship questions — it was making her feel sad, and she was none the wiser. She would need to pay the magic man a visit, then she remembered — that was something she'd planned to do with John and Jean.

'If you don't mind me asking, how do you make a living? Only it seems quite an idyllic lifestyle, well, maybe apart from no Wi-Fi. I was wondering how you afford to eat, travel, get about . . . you know?' She remembered his kind gestures of coffee, snacks, treating her to a curry, and not least the two nights' stay in the Atlantis Hotel. 'It's something I've wondered from time to time while I've been here. Oh, maybe you have a hotbed of these Atlantis stones?'

She turned to look out along the horizon, not wanting him to look too closely in case he picked up on other things she was wondering about.

'I had my own business, a while ago now. It was a type of consultancy, giving financial advice. Sometimes over the phone, or other times online or one-to-one meetings — ugh! It was going really well — in fact, too well.'

'Well that was a good thing, surely?'

Serena had known there was more to him than first appeared. He was a numbers whizz, and probably made lots of dosh and had it all banked away for a rainy day. She listened attentively.

'I decided to opt out in the end ... too many false friends hanging on. I left the wheeling and dealing to the others. Only on my rare trips back to the UK, it's not long before the phone calls start. And they'll go anything along the lines of, 'Can you tell me ... ?' or 'Have you got any tips ... insider knowledge ... blah, blah, and bloody blah'?' He physically recoiled, looking as if someone had given him terrible news.

Serena felt a pain in the pit of her stomach. Watching his face and knowing how he must be agonising over his past, she could now partly begin to understand why he might want to be a recluse. He came across as an intelligent man; she could imagine how popular he would be back in the city. He was a good listener, and gave good advice. After only a day on the island, she had witnessed the patience he showed to his friend's children, the respect he bestowed on Cindy and he treated Agwe like a brother, even though they wrestled like crazy beasts on occasion.

I wonder what he thinks of me. Am I only someone to keep him company for a while and then . . . Well, what then? That was the thing; they hadn't spoken any deeper than having jambalaya for supper and swimming with dolphins.

They clambered over a rocky part of the beach which opened out onto a secluded cove. Broderick pointed out a stream of silver humps arching their way across the sparkling water.

'There really are dolphins! Lots of them. This is a dream come true for me.' Serena shielded her eyes and gasped as more splashing and tail slapping occurred.

The only previous time she'd seen dolphins was on holiday with her family at Cardigan Bay. But there weren't as many as this — and now they were playing and making strange noises.

'Broderick, do you think they know we're here?'

She watched him cup his hands around his mouth. She listened as he communicated with the mammals, in a cross between a cry and a quack, an eerie sound that drove the sea creatures wild.

'Look, they're doing acrobatics. Is it safe to go in the water with them — can we?'

He nodded and pointed out rocky remains of a man-made causeway that jutted out into the waves. 'Make your way along there and then they'll come right up to you. I'll join you in a minute. Let me use your camera. It's a good photo opportunity for you, and they'll be pictures to add to your portfolio.'

Feeling shy for a moment, she reminded herself realising she'd already seen him stark naked, so what was a red

flowery bikini to worry about? Antici-
pating that they might go swimming,
she'd worn it under her clothes.

Stepping out of her shorts and
pulling her top off, she put her clothes
in a heap on the beach. 'Will they be all
right there?'

Broderick nodded. She couldn't help
noticing the way he glanced at her legs
and didn't look too disappointed. She
smiled in spite of herself, walked
steadily over the shingle and onto the
rocky causeway, taking her time, and
then stepping delicately onto the path.

Serena stood tall, waved as he took
her photograph, and then dived grace-
fully into the aquamarine ocean. She
found herself touching noses with a
baby dolphin, who almost shovelled her
up onto his back like a playful big dog.
Her shrieks matched the sounds of the
mammals and Broderick joined in the
fun from the beach with his dolphin
cry. Not for the first time this holiday,
Serena thought life could never get any
better than this.

She counted six of the gorgeous creatures who circled and dived, seemingly having as much fun as she was.

'They're adorable!' she called. She swam and cooed as the tip of the larger silver dolphin's nose touched her own and he made a gentle sound that was a mixture of a high pitched squeal and a duck's quack. She sent an exaggerated smile across to Broderick who'd already lined up her camera and began capturing more shots of the fun-filled moment.

'Come on in.' She bobbed up from the water and threw him a high wave, tossing her braids behind her shoulders. 'I'd like to take some pictures of you,' she shouted across the water.

Immediately her mind drifted back to the shower moment and she kicked herself for not grabbing a picture then, when she had chance!

He secured the camera and her other belongings behind a rock before he shook off his boots. Serena couldn't avert her gaze as she watched him quickly remove his Bermuda shorts to reveal navy briefs. He shook his shirt off and left his clothes to fall in a heap on the sand then took great strides along the pathway before flipping into a backward dive much the same as the dolphins. He surfaced only a foot away from her.

'They're tame, aren't they?' Broderick touched noses with one of the smaller dolphins which made a laughing sound and flipped backwards, looking for all the world like a puppy playing with his best friend.

'I can see now how you'd never be lonely out here.' She trod water and lifted her face to the sky, wondering how she'd found paradise.

He was beside her in the water and suddenly dived deep down, then hoisted her up for a piggy back ride.

'This is the best way to get among them. Hold on tight.' She gasped as he shook his hair and sent a cascade of sea spray over her face, and then he swooped and dived in the water giving her no option other than to quickly wind her legs firmly around his waist and fix her hands onto his broad shoulders. The closeness of his firm body against her own made her tingle, and her shrieks of laughter were a mixture of excitement and sheer joy.

Serena buried her face into the back of his neck and closed her eyes, breathing in the scent of freedom and the most manly man she'd ever come across in her life. She brushed her lips across the back of his broad shoulders and moaned softly before she screamed out, 'Oh, yes, the dolphins are fantastic!'

In truth, the attraction of the dolphins had become secondary — but she knew she'd never come close to having any moments like this ever again if she lived to be a hundred.

11

Kathleen-Miranda Beckingsworth was used to having her own way, and for over a year, she'd been trying to talk sense into Lord Broderick Loveday.

'Imagine how much easier things would be if only we were to get married? Aileen would have a proper daddy, and we could be invited to parties and special events.'

Seeing as he was deaf to everything she said, and insisted that he was already Aileen's proper daddy, she knew her only option was to travel to the Caribbean and sort this little problem out before things got out of hand.

Secretly, she imagined a better life for herself, consumed with thoughts like . . . *I'll be asked to open garden fêtes and be able to turn up in a big hat and wear gorgeous dresses. Not to mention all those lunch parties that people with connections throw. As a family, we'll probably become the new celebs on the high street.*

Kathleen had visions of their daughter mixing with children of A-listers and other high flyers. Not that she or even Broderick were celebs yet, but people always clamoured to talk to him. He had that certain something that attracted women — and men — like a magnet, yet he never even tried to make anything of himself. He just had the X factor. Her daughter would have more influential friends, and their life would be ten times better than it was now — if only he could see sense and ask her to marry him.

She'd think about it of course, for a few minutes and then jump into his arms, and say, 'Yes.'

Pity he was such a stubborn old independent idiot when it came to romance. Yet he had fancied her once, Aileen was living proof of that . . . even if she had been the one doing most of the seducing.

A multi-coloured macaw sat on a branch outside Kathleen's window at the Atlantis hotel. She wasn't accustomed to being chatted up by a parrot, and leaned out of the window to tell him to fly away. She glanced at her watch. Only half an hour until she met the local lads who were willing to help her make progress with her plans.

The map lay open on her bedside table, and X marked the spot. There was treasure to be found; even though she wasn't sure what it was, it was bound to be important, otherwise he'd never have marked it.

She tutted. Typical! Subtle as a bucket of horse manure, playing at being Desert Island Danny when all along he could be in London.

Our picture could be on the front of every magazine and newspaper, me draped across his arm, him gazing lovingly at me.

Glancing at her reflection in the mirror, she knew how the plans should be working out. Now she'd come all this way, she would do all in her power to get the results she wanted and finally make him see sense.

After all, she had the ace of hearts in her possession in the form of their daughter, and that would clear a path to talking him round sooner or later. He couldn't play the recluse forever. How did that saying go . . . no man is an island?

★   ★   ★

Shami and Rhawand pulled into the harbour and secured their boat before jumping out and climbing the steps of the jetty and making their way along to the promenade. They were supposed to meet the English lady by Davy Jones' Locker, and they felt sure she would pay well. She promised she would when she'd roughly mentioned what she wanted them to do. If finding treasure that was clearly marked, and somewhere on the Island of Shells, was all it was, then this job would be a doddle.

They wouldn't even have to involve the Blackeye Wanderers, who were the big guys when it came to undercover jobs. Often they were the ones who settled the deals and Shami and Rhawand were only the errand boys. Now it was time to prove they could go it alone.

★   ★   ★

She was sitting under the lemon grove, by the pub doorway, sipping a drink from a pint glass with coloured straws bent over the edge. Her large brimmed hat and oversized sunglasses didn't hide the English lady here in the Caribbean on the hunt for hidden treasure.

Of course, what she really wanted was the man himself, but until he came to his senses and realised their getting together was inevitable, she would have to make do with the alternative.

The young buccaneers sat opposite, waiting for instructions.

'You were going to discuss what you

wanted us to do.' Shami leaned his elbows on the table, eager to get down to business. 'And we know the place you talk about like it was our own back yard.' He gave a devilish smile.

'So, if I said there's treasure where that X marks the spot, you'd know where to look?' Kathleen pushed the paper across the table towards them and leaned back in her chair. 'Does that diagram make any sense to you?'

Minor irritation tinged her voice. She wondered if it might be too much of a risk, asking a pair of island drop-outs to help, but they wouldn't need paying too much. If they managed to come up with the goods, she'd be satisfied . . . and Lord Loveday might at last sit up and take notice of her if she had his precious treasure.

The Buccaneers looked at the map and worked out that the cross was somewhere in the shrubbery area of the island. That part where the lush greenery was hard to get through, but the stream, marked on the map with a blue dotted line made with a felt pen, told them it was more over to the back of the Englishman's camp.

'I'm going to get Sky-Blou to give us a hand. She'll know exactly where this is, but she'll be our excuse if we get caught. You know . . . ' Shami tilted his head and winked at his friend. 'Thing is, if me and you get caught snooping around near that geezer's base camp, he might smell a rat.

'Now if we get caught with a couple of girls, or say if I'm with Sky-Blou and you're just tagging along, as you do, then nothing much will be said . . . other than clear off and behave, usual stuff.' He gave a salacious grin. The pair made a high five and a fist bump. Their mission — to find buried treasure — was underway. They had faces like full moons as they heard Kathleen shout after them.

'Don't forget, you only get the payment in full when I get my hands on that treasure.'

'What is the treasure, did she say?'

Rhawand wanted to know.

Shami frowned. 'No, she didn't, now you come to say. Bet she doesn't even know herself. I'm thinking jewellery, or money, antiques . . . must be valuable or she wouldn't be paying us half the money up front, now, would she?'

'And how much is she paying us, then?' Rhawand, the youngest of the pair, wanted to make sure the risk of getting caught would be worth his while.

'For cripes sakes, why didn't you speak up while we were with her then?' Shami was secretly kicking himself for not getting the deal done properly. Now they might need to have a chat with the Blackeye Wanderers after all.

It was a sheepish pair who pulled alongside the low harbour wall on Shark Island further south. They made their way to the local pub where Danny Monsoon always played his card games.

He pushed his cigar into the ash tray when the boys approached.

'Hello lads . . . What's new, you found something interesting for me?'

His bad teeth were almost falling from his mouth as his trademark sneer spread across his face. The lads weren't completely afraid of him, but the thought of him finding out they'd been moonlighting was enough to sober their thoughts. And he had at his disposal an island full of men who he called to hand whenever he needed them — his gang, the Blackeye Wanderers.

'Thing is, it's like this . . . '

Over half an hour later, Shami and Rhawand came away with the promise of a hundred pounds each if they went along with Kathleen's plan, but kept Danny — head of the Blackeye Wanderers informed.

'You're a dim-wit, man!' Rhawand clasped his mate under the crux of his arm, bending him forward and threatening to throw him into the sea. 'What's the first rule of doing a deal? Do the bloody deal; honestly, sometimes I think I should go solo.'

Shami wriggled free. 'Be my guest, and how far do you think you'd get without my brains?'

Running towards his friend, they tussled and wrestled each other until they eventually went over the side of the bank and sank to the sandy sea bed. Surfacing almost as quickly as they'd gone down, they laughed loudly and swam back to the boat. If either of them was disappointed, it didn't show. They were small-time bounty hunters, and with the backing of old man Blackeye, it would be a doddle.

* * *

After swimming with dolphins, the afternoon mellowed into one long hazy delightful blur for Serena. During the long walk along the sand, she absent-mindedly clasped Broderick's hand, and he didn't make any attempt to pull away. They casually swung their arms, fingers entwined, as they walked and talked about the evening and Broderick mentioned that he planned to cater for quite a crowd.

'I cook for Agwe and his family, and then they do the same for me another time. Only occasionally I eat alone.' He glanced at Serena and she couldn't help thinking it was such a waste — him being single and on his own.

'It's good to share the cooking, and I really can't wait to try the jambalaya.' She grinned, and then placed her hand on her reddening shoulder. 'Oh, I almost forgot . . . time for the sunblock again.' Reaching into her bag, she pulled out the factor fifty that she'd bought with her. Plastering it over her face and arms, she attempted to put some around the back of her neck.

'Here, let me.' Broderick took the bottle of lotion from her and gently rubbed the cream into the back of her neck, making circular movements onto her shoulders down her arms and across her exposed back, and then he rubbed some more sun cream down where the top of her bikini bottom skimmed . . . he glanced for only a moment.

He quickly moved his hand back up to her shoulders and neck, making sure every part of her skin was protected from the sun. When he'd finished, Broderick dipped his head close to her neck, managing to avoid making a fool of himself. He closed his eyes to block out the vision of the woman he was coming to know so well, then cleared his throat and clipped the bottle shut.

'There, all done. Well and truly protected.'

From the sun, he chided himself, feeling dizzy from the rush of emotion that had threatened to overwhelm him at the feel of her warm skin beneath his fingers. *Stop thinking of Serena and making love on the sand . . . stop it now!*

'Thank you, shall I do the same for you?'

Her smile was sweet and the way she was looking at him caused his insides to somersault, making his heart lurch. He wanted her more with every passing minute. This had to end right now. He was a desert islander; this was meant to be a moment of fun, not getting involved and certainly no physical relationships. Nothing like this was needed in his life right now. Only the thought of his Aileen put him back on track.

'I'm all right, thanks — quite used to the weather, and I have my hat.' He grinned and slung his weather-resistant headgear across the back of his neck. 'Come on, there's good foraging to be had on these hills, then we can double back to camp.' He took her hand and put all thoughts of kissing her all over to the back of his mind.

As they rounded another high-sided cliff, the beach broke into a grass pathway and in the distance, Serena saw palm trees laid out on a small terrace. Music drifted across and the sound of distant laughter carried on the breeze.

'Ah, is that some kind of civilisation I

see? And there was me thinking this was a completely deserted island other than you and a handful of locals.'

He smiled. 'We have a market and good foraging, as I said.'

Further along, piles of tomatoes and other vegetables were piled high on the floor and farm animals wandered among the stalls.

After more delicious coffee in the market café, and gathering all the ingredients needed for the supper, which seemed to cost very little, the two of them took a different route back to camp.

'There are more people on the island than I first thought.' She had taken some pictures of the goats and chickens running around the market.

'Some folk arrive for market day, set up their stall, and then hop back over to another island when they know they can sell their goods. You'd be amazed at the business skills of the Caribbean folk. They're not all reggae-loving pot smokers, you know.'

She knew he was teasing, and gave him a gentle shove. Why did she ever have to go back to the real world when all she wanted to do was stay here with her island man forever?

12

Anything I can do to help?' Serena asked politely.

Broderick looked to have the evening's supper he was preparing for his guests in hand, but she wanted to make herself useful. She knew where the herbs grew that he'd told her he would be using.

'If you like, I could gather some of those herbs and salad leaves you mentioned. And I'm sure you'll need a bay leaf.' She grinned, remembering his mantra; *if in doubt, add a bay leaf.*

'It's pretty well all on the go now.' He swung round to face her. 'The preparing doesn't take that long. You can gather some wild garlic as well, if you don't mind. And you're right; a few bay leaves are always useful.' He smiled, and Serena noticed again the crinkles around his eyes and how much darker

207

his skin had become since she'd first met him on the plane.

'The ingredients we bought from the market are coming on a treat, simmering and softening.' He prodded and stirred at the concoction in the huge pan with a wooden spoon as he spoke. 'We could go together. That's unless you wanted some time to yourself?' He glanced across to where she was selecting a wicker basket from the pile of containers stacked up against the makeshift cupboard.

She swung around, shocked that he could think such a thing. 'Absolutely not; I didn't want to drag you away from your cooking, but if you reckon it'll be all right?'

Walking towards him, she sniffed the air over the huge cauldron of chicken, sausage and vegetable jambalaya. 'Mmm, smells divine. Surely most of the ingredients must be in there now?' She glanced at the blend of colourful chunks of meat and vegetables.

Broderick held a sample of rich-looking sauce on a spoon to her mouth. Their eyes met as she sipped and she hoped he couldn't read how she felt about him after such a short time, or see the slight tremble in her fingers as they brushed against his.

Most guys she'd met before would by now have tried something. He was different.

Maybe he just doesn't fancy me — or women at all, for that matter.

Serena fought back her disappointment. She felt a special magnetism between them whenever he was near. She dreamed of them making love beneath the Caribbean sky to the sound of the sea lapping against the shore. It was how he made her feel — but, accepting this wasn't likely to happen, she pushed all such thoughts to the back of her mind.

'We only have to catch the shrimps. Here, grab this . . . ' The fishing net he threw in her direction was still damp from the day before, and had a whiff of stale fish.

Serena wrinkled her nose and grasped it.

'Couldn't we have got some in the market when we bought the other items?'

She hadn't quite got the hang of catching her supper, though it was becoming a habit, going to the edge of the rock pools to look for something good enough to eat. As long as she was spending time with her own Robinson Crusoe, she didn't mind putting up with a few tasks she normally wouldn't dream of doing.

Wild rocket leaves were the first item she found growing near a stream, and wild garlic was so pungent they need only follow the trail. Broderick assured her they would make all the difference. He led the way to the maze of rock pools, where the late afternoon sun sent an amber veil across the water.

'There's a giant crab under there as well.' Broderick leaned over a huge grey boulder. 'See that shadow?' His eyes twinkled. 'He's watching the bait, and they can never resist a small chunk of corned beef. Watch this now.'

He lay completely still, eyes squinted and tongue gently curled up against the side of his lip, gently dragging the bait across the bottom of the boulder to tempt the shell fish from his den.

In one stealthy movement he swung the crab up and then firmly clasped it on either edge of the oval shell to watch its pincers going like crazy trying to nip anything that came in the way before dropping it straight into the waiting bucket.

★   ★   ★

Shami and Rhawand used oars to steer their boat quietly into the rushes on the western side of the Island of Shells.

'Is Sky-Blou meeting you like she promised? I never trust a girl as pretty as that one.'

'Erm, yes, Rhawand, and knowing the zero amount of pretty girls you've been involved with, what would you know about my gorgeous girl?'

'Didn't know she was your girl. Bet she's only interested in free ferry crossings if you ask me.'

'Well I didn't ask you, and speak of the most beautiful girl on the island, here she comes now.' He gave Rhawand a shove to keep him from saying anything more stupid than he already had and gave a low whistle as Sky-Blou parted the bushes and walked out of the shrubbery.

'Are we still looking for treasure? Only thing is, I've been invited to a banquet later — well, an island type of gathering, which will go on until late tonight probably.'

Sky-Blou linked arms with Shami and batted her eyelashes. Rhawand turned away.

'Yes my lovely, and here's the map.' Finding the nearest rock, Shami smoothed it out and showed her where X marked the spot. 'I'm banking on you helping us to find the exact place,

212

but it's up some hills there by the looks of the markings.'

Sky-Blou nodded. 'What are we looking for, do you know?' She tilted her head. 'Only if it's something dodgy, my dad wouldn't want me getting involved. He knows you take me across the water, but if this is shady business . . . '

'As if I'd ever put you in danger! You've upset me now.' He dropped his chin to his chest and pulled a little-boy sad face. Noticing she wasn't responding, he said, 'OK, I wouldn't expect an invite to the supper, but come on, there's time to find this treasure before your family and friends start to mingle around.'

He handed the treasure map over to Sky-Blou who looked up to the late afternoon sky, using the sun as a compass.

'I'd say we need to head inland and in an easterly direction.' Sky Blou felt secretly proud that the Caribbean buccaneers were enlisting her help. She knew they wouldn't have a clue without her, and it was her first big adventure.

Stealing a backward glance to check they were keeping up, she waved them on. In a half whisper — she didn't know why, other than that it made the adventure more exciting — she said, 'Be careful of the brambles ahead, there are nettles as well.'

With a toss of her head, she led the way, feeling every inch a pirate princess. All that was missing was a dagger for chopping down brambles. Her dad would never agree to her carrying a weapon.

★   ★   ★

Broderick flicked his eyes towards the lush greenery on the edge of the mountainous part of the island. He'd heard the mock bird call.

He knew every sound in the place where he felt safe and the arrival of the kids didn't bother him, but the fact that they hadn't shown themselves to say hello piqued his interest.

He watched and listened as the distant crack of a branch and the glint of late sun on their makeshift scythes as they chopped a pathway to the direction of the lagoon highlighted their path.

He placed a finger to his lips when Serena gave him a concerned frown. The hint of a wink he gave her let her know that he wasn't concerned, more intrigued.

'Is it usual for them to arrive on the island and go hiking?' She felt a cold shiver and couldn't help remember her earlier encounter with the buccaneers. 'What are they doing up there? Surely they're not hunting, or . . . ' Her mind was going into overdrive. 'They might be looking for someone, please don't tell me they've come to find me and escort me back to the mainland or something daft like that? And they needn't think of robbing me because all I've got is my laptop and camera.' She didn't think to bring them with her to the rock pools; she presumed they'd be safe back at base camp.

Broderick gave a low chuckle. 'Perhaps they've been hired by that magazine you're supposed to be working for?' He raised an eyebrow and turned away.

Slapping her palm to her forehead, Serena gasped. 'Oh Lord, the drunken monkeys, I must get on to that immediately. That was the point of coming here in the first place.' She scanned his bronzed body and admired his legs in his shorts.

Would it break all the rules in the book if I just leaned across and gave him . . . ? But knowing my luck we'd fall flat on our faces into the rock pool.

As she was considering tasting his lips rather than the jambalaya, he reached for her hand. Serena felt his grey eyes fixated on her lips and she wondered if he might kiss her. She felt a tingling sensation, really hoping he would, but wasn't surprised when he flicked his eyes away and squeezed her hand.

'I'd like to read you some poetry, but let's get these back to base and finish cooking first.'

It was starting to get cooler; Broderick gave her a helping hand to step along the right boulders to get safely back onto the beach. Serena couldn't help thinking what a gentleman he was. Would she ever have got to know him this intimately if she'd met him in other circumstances, back in London or somewhere else in the United Kingdom?

Noticing he still had an eye on the two lads and the girl doing their best to stay camouflaged on their trek, she noticed a cold shiver running down her spine for the second time recently.

13

You're quite safe with me; don't worry about being scalped by those kids.' Broderick patted the makeshift bench to the side of him, indicating for her to join him. 'Supper is keeping warm over the fire.'

When he saw the panic etched across Serena's face, he laughed as he reassured her.

'Relax, I'm kidding, they're really only probably playing boy scouts or something. They know I'm down here, so if they were up to no good, they'd be prowling around in the middle of the night — not early evening.'

Broderick was secretly more worried than he was letting on and he could tell that for some reason, she wasn't reassured. He remembered her reaction when Agwe had crept up with his attack moves. She had a vivid imagination

— maybe because she was a reporter. He needed to work harder at keeping her calm.

The last thing he wanted was a crazy journalist roaming about and reporting exaggerated stories back to the papers. It crossed his mind that he knew one way to distract her completely, but that was quite inappropriate — and the last thing he wanted was a relationship to complicate his simple life. So he pushed all images of her swimming in that skimpy bikini to the back of his mind.

'Are you warm enough?' He put his arm loosely round her shoulders and gave her a hug. 'These will make you feel better . . . ' He placed a couple of cushions behind her, and then gave her a sideways glance and a shy smile before scooping up his poetry collection. 'Now, make yourself comfortable.' He began to read from his favourite book once more.

Serena smiled then closed her eyes as she listened to his melodic voice and the distant swish of the waves, both having the soothing effect she needed. He read about love, nature and all things beautiful, making her wish she could be more honest about her feelings for him.

Then she checked herself, and sat up quickly knowing it wouldn't be long before his extended family would be arriving for supper. Quite apart from that, she didn't feel easy knowing the buccaneers were roaming the hillside.

★ ★ ★

Up near the lagoon, the trio were arguing about what they were hoping to achieve.

'It's not right!' Sky-Blou made a fist with her left hand and rested it on her hip. 'You're only using me to get what you want, and I know it's to do with Broderick's belongings because this is his private place. I thought the adventure was a bit of fun and make-believe, not rummaging around looking for other people's treasures. When you mentioned jewels I thought you meant old buried stuff, not things belonging to us on the island.'

'Who mentioned gems?' The lads looked blankly at each other. They had no clue as to what they were looking for. 'You must have imagined that, babe. There could be gems, but nobody told me.' Shami gave a half-hearted shrug.

'You agreed to help us, babe, why the cold feet now?' Shami tilted his head sideways and pleaded with his girl, his eyes imploring. 'There's dollar in it for all of us if we just get to the point and find the treasure.' He waved his hands around and began to get twitchy.

'Look, the last thing we need is for you to go cold and raise the alarm. So far so good, we only need another ten or fifteen minutes and then we'll scarper with the booty. Nobody will be any the wiser.'

He looked at the map again, checking the markings and screwing his eyes up to see what was directly in line where the arrow was pointing.

'The waterfall, it's right in line with the treasure.' Shami looked at the other two.

Sky-Blou stood firm. 'No, this doesn't feel right. And besides, it's time for me to go for the supper now. Here is as far as I go.' She turned. 'And don't call me babe.'

The smell of the jambalaya was drifting up through the trees and she followed her nose, glad to be away from the pair of clowns who were up to no good. No money or gem was worth getting into trouble with her dad, and she began to feel sick in her stomach at the thought of them doing harm to Broderick or his private property.

She wished now that she hadn't got involved and knew she had to put things right — preferably without getting into trouble herself, though it was a bit late for that. She made a quick getaway and prayed they wouldn't follow her. She knew deep down they had no backbone and was certain they wouldn't want to face her dad or Broderick.

Once out of their line of vision, Sky-Blou ran as fast as she could back down to the safety of the general tracks, where she bumped headlong into her mam and dad on their way to supper in Camp Broderick. She could only stammer at first and then ended blurting it all out.

'Dad, I'm sorry, they're up there and looking for some treasure. You need to stop them, and I have to warn Broderick. It's my fault, they used me, and Dad, you were right about them all along.' Her face crumpled. She bit hard on her lower lip to stop herself from crying, but it didn't work.

Agwe cast a worried glance in the direction his daughter had come running from.

'They haven't hurt you, sweetheart? Because I warned him . . . ' He held Sky-Blou gently by the shoulders and looked into her tear-streaked face. 'Tell me the truth now, because I will find out.'

Her mother came forward and hugged her.

'Mam, Dad, nothing happened like that — they wanted me to show them a place on an old map. It's something to do with Broderick.'

A rustle in the undergrowth made them all stop and turn.

★ ★ ★

The campfire burned low; Broderick put his book to one side and got up to throw a hefty log across the embers and a couple of smaller ones. 'There, that'll keep it going while we wait for the others to arrive.' He smiled and Serena stood up to join him as he walked to where there was a sea view between the trees.

Then he gave a low whistle and turned to her, eyes wide.

'The Blackeye Wanderers, aboard The Ruby Queen of the Caribbean, if

I'm not mistaken,' he whispered. Reaching for a pair of binoculars, he adjusted them and held them to his eyes. 'Drat, things just got a bit more dangerous, but keep calm, Serena — nothing we can't handle, eh?'

He was looking her as if she was supposed to complete her transformation into Jane of the Jungle.

'Let me have a look.' She took the binoculars he was offering her. 'Wow — that stunning boat out there, you mean? It's the Ruby Queen — or is it a woman on the boat you're talking about?'

'Of course the ship, magnificent vessel, it's an old galleon they've refurbished, but full of pirates, and forget your Johnny Depp stereotype; these are full-time badass men of the sea.' He cast a quick glance in her direction. 'Come on, we have to go and find the kids. There's more to their visit than a bit of exploring, something doesn't smell right.' He grabbed her hand and swept her along as he strode towards the hills.

Half running, half jogging, Serena could hardly keep up. Then they heard the shouting — Sky-Blou insisting she hadn't been hurt. Broderick and Serena burst through the shrubbery, as they heard her telling them it was something belonging to Broderick they were looking for.

'Tell me exactly where they are — if you can remember.' He spoke with a rasping urgency that seemed quite out of character.

Sky-Blou looked frightened and spoke quietly now. The tremor in her voice betrayed her nervousness. 'We had got to the waterfall; they were interested in looking closer, I think. That's when I ran off.' She cast her eyes to the ground, and reached for her mother's hand.

Agwe gave Broderick a nudge and for a nano-second, Serena saw his eyes flick to the ocean. Without saying anything, he'd let his best friend know that the Ruby Queen of the Caribbean was in sight. A brief nod was the reply from

Broderick. Now Serena's heart was beating faster and she wondered if the pirates would be coming ashore. She really hoped not — and she didn't want that pot of scrumptious jambalaya to go to waste.

Broderick must have read her mind when he said, 'Why don't you go on back to camp now, and get the plates out ready for supper. This won't take long.' He pulled his head to one side, gesturing for Agwe to accompany him further up the hill, starting on the track without her.

Serena grabbed his hand and pulled herself level with him. 'I've come this far in to the wilderness, you're not getting rid of me now.' She raised her chin and looked directly into his grey eyes, daring him to contradict. 'You do know what century we're in? Just because there's a pirate ship on the horizon, and some scallywags around, I'm not likely to faint or throw a wobbly — '

Sky-Blou was tittering behind her. A jabbering sound and more rustling made Serena turn round. A small, furry ball of screaming monkey grabbed her camera, scampered across the path and shimmied up the nearest tree, then let out a chattering that had everyone looking upward.

'Could that be a drunken monkey?' Serena clasped Broderick's hand and turned to Sky-Blou. 'That's the reason I've come all this way, to send stories about the drunken monkeys in the Caribbean. And now he's taking pictures of us!'

'If he's been round my dad's punch bowl then he could be quite blotto . . .'

The group of friends were suddenly bombarded with a shower of fruit.

'It's raining guavas! Take cover.' Broderick made a chattering sound that replicated the noise the creature had made a moment ago. He stood under the tree and opened his arms, still chattering. Serena watched, open-mouthed, as he coaxed the monkey down and gently took her camera from him. He threw it back to her and gestured to her to follow.

'If you insist, then come on. We're wasting time, and no chance of making a discreet advance on the buccaneers with this fellow nattering away.' He slung the monkey onto his back and it rode with head held high as if it had known Broderick for years.

'You didn't think to mention that there was a resident drunken money on this island?' Serena was slightly miffed. 'To think I could have been getting my articles written and you've kept this one quiet. Does he have a name?' She refused to hold Broderick's hand, keeping a tight grip on her camera that she wore around her neck.

Broderick put a finger to his lips. 'There are monkeys everywhere,' he whispered, 'you just didn't look hard enough. And I'm not doing your work for you; if you were a proper journalist you'd find a story anywhere.'

So now I know exactly what he thinks of me . . . so why am I wasting my time here?

Then again, it's not often this kind of thing happens to me. Let's face it, the only excitement I've had in years was when the photocopier machine broke down at work and that hunky bloke came to fix it.

Cindy shouted after her husband, 'Agwe, me and the kids will go back to Broderick's and lay the food out.' She rounded up the children who had now caught up with her. The boys were wanting to follow their father. 'No — you'll come with me, and keep a watch out for pirates. That's a really important job, isn't it, Agwe? Tell them.' She waited.

'Your mam needs you to look after her.'

He winked at his wife, who smiled, glad that he was able to keep control of the younger ones.

Cindy linked arms with Sky-Blou and made a promise to herself to get her to talk about this fledgling relationship that wasn't doing her daughter any favours.

14

As they walked, Serena took photos of the new addition to the party. He rode on Broderick's shoulders and looked more like a barn owl than a monkey the way he swivelled his head to watch her, even giving a comical smile for the camera.

She made wide eyes and smiled back at him and he chattered even louder. She'd swear he wore a conceited look as if he might be thinking, *I'm getting carried up the hill, and you're not.*

As they neared the lagoon, it came to Serena's mind that in other circumstances, she and Broderick might have come back here alone. In her fantasy, they might have bathed under the waterfall, but now it was more of a mystery adventure. At least she was glad Sky-Blou was with her family, out of harm's way.

Agwe and Broderick crouched down and indicated for her to do the same. Even the monkey lay flat across the grass between the two men. Serena hardly dared breathe in case she had a coughing fit or said something stupid. She swallowed hard and crouched beside them.

This was deadly serious. Knowing there was a pirate ship anchored in the bay gave her the creeps. She'd heard locals talk about the ruthless baddies known as the Blackeye Wanderers, and for all she knew they might be planning to invade the island. What if they took Broderick away?

A cold fear gripped her entire body. Her heart began banging against her ribcage; she had to do something to help. Simply following them around wasn't helping. All she wanted to do was stay near Broderick — she felt safe around him, even if he made insulting remarks without seeming to realise he'd offended her sometimes.

'OK, what's behind the falls, on the

map? They're going to a lot of trouble to dig up something valuable.' Agwe lifted himself up on his elbows and looked Broderick in the eye.

'So that's it . . . ' Broderick raised his eyes and breathed out heavily. 'They've got my rough sketch map, so now we know.' He whispered, 'I keep things hidden behind the waterfall as nobody goes over there, only me. There's only one person who could have found that . . . I thought I'd thrown the original draft away. Blast — she better hadn't be anywhere near here.'

Agwe looked astonished.

'Kathleen is behind this, you mean?' He knew the history and trouble his mate was constantly trying to escape from every time he came to the Caribbean. 'Sky-Blou mentioned a map before she left with her mam. What treasure lies beyond the falls? And where did they get that map? You need to ask some questions.' He shifted his position to get a closer look and to see Shami and Rhawand reaching through the boulders, getting a soaking into the bargain.

'The map will be sodden by now, and it's my guess they don't even know what they're looking for. But you can bet the Blackeye Wanderers are involved in this. What have you got hidden, then?'

Agwe wouldn't let it go and Serena piped up.

'What a stupid idea, hiding valuables outdoors. Anyone could go there, and they are — right now.'

She whispered so loud it came out as a squeak. 'Haven't you heard of safe deposit boxes?'

Broderick drew in a deep breath and then quietly told them both, 'Let them carry on a while longer. They're going nowhere — even if they do find what they're looking for.'

'What about the pirate ship? Is it staying there, waiting for these lads? It's getting too dangerous now. Surely we should call the police, or the coast-guards?' Serena persisted.

Agwe almost choked on the piece of sugar cane he was chewing.

'Aw, man, you're cute.' He gave a broad grin and shook his head as if he'd heard a really good joke when all she was doing was trying to get some sense into the situation.

'Well, surely we ought . . . ' She didn't have time to finish as Broderick hollered across the ridge.

'Right! Hold it there, you've done enough snooping and stealing. I'll take a look at what you've found.'

He stood up and was looking across towards Shami who clutched a wad of paper to his chest. Like a flash, Broderick pulled off his boots and dived into the navy water. As he moved, the monkey jumped equally quickly and landed aboard his shoulders. Broderick didn't even flinch.

'But I didn't think they liked . . . ' Serena wanted to say it wouldn't be safe for the little monkey but as she watched him clinging onto Broderick's back, it all looked perfectly normal.

Broderick gave a deft flick of his long hair as he swam, the monkey clinging to his back. He made fast work of reaching the other side and then scrambled up the rocks to where the lads were standing like rabbits caught in head-lights.

'Who sent you?'

He pinned Shami up against the rock-face.

Serena was taken by surprise — but not so much as Rhawand was, when Agwe dropped down from above and held him tightly. He'd taken the rugged route around the back of the waterfall, and tiptoed up unseen. The two lads had plenty of chance to pull out their knives, but Broderick was puma-fast and grabbed Shami's wrist, took the knife and the one Rhawand had dropped then kicked them with the side of his sock-covered foot down into the water. He held Shami in an armlock and took the papers from his grasp.

Serena hadn't even seen Agwe move from the spot, and Broderick moved like a panther in the dusk light. She was in awe of the agility of the two men, and felt completely helpless being there as an onlooker. She glanced behind her, feeling nervous. Then she had a brainwave and reached for her camera. She fired off a string of photographs, wishing help would come.

Shouting over to the men, she asked, 'Do you want me to go for help?'

Argh, who would I go to for assistance, when the two toughest men around are already apprehending the intruders?

'Call the monkey; he answers to Chunky when he wants something.' Broderick lifted the creature from his shoulders with one hand, while continuing to restrain Shami, and appeared to whisper in its ear.

'Come here, Chunky, come on . . . ' Serena whistled to the chattering monkey, taking pictures as he swung down the flimsy trees growing from the rocks and took the stepping stone route further down the lagoon. 'What will he do — go and get reinforcements, and bring the police or coastguards?'

She could feel the cold, hard stare Broderick sent from across the water.

'No — he's coming to fetch my boots.'

Well, how was I to know the monkey is yet another of Broderick Loveday's loyal helpers?

* * *

John and Jean were enjoying a relaxing glass of wine on the terrace of the hotel after another lovely day. Only one thing was bothering them, and that was, what had happened to Serena?

'She was all for going to see the Ju Ju man with us, and it seems a bit strange that she hasn't popped in to say hello.' Jean reached for a handful of salted peanuts from the bowl on the table.

'I know . . . like I was saying, one of the boatmen told me she'd gone over to one of the small islands to explore.' John took a swig of wine and rubbed the back of his hand across his chin.

Tutting and shaking her head, Jean couldn't hide the frown that formed across her brow.

'I know it's a different age now, love, but somehow . . . I don't know, it really doesn't seem right, a young woman going off alone on a ferry boat. She needs to be careful. I'm worried, John — something could have happened to her.'

'Maybe if we popped down to the harbour and asked around, how does that sound? It's true as you said, it's a different world now, what with all the internet and social media she's probably busy with her laptop if I had to guess. Everyone has their head buried in a phone or laptops these days, don't they?'

'Let's not guess, we'll do what you suggested — take a walk down the harbourside and ask around.' Jean pulled on a shawl, fluffed her hair into her favourite style, sprayed on some Anaïs Anaïs, then smiled at her husband.

'Well, you know I like to look presentable,' she explained. 'We're acting as undercover detectives. People will talk more freely if we're presentable, and smelling fragrant goes a long way in my book. I was wondering though, John, whether we ought to inform the local police. Or we could let them know we're concerned. I mean, if anything happened . . . ' She gripped her hand to her chest. 'I'd never forgive myself.'

John nodded. The last thing he would dream of doing was disagreeing with Jean. He'd known his wife since their high school days and as long as she was happy, he was happy.

'Let's go and ask around first, then if we see or hear anything to arouse suspicion, we could mention her not being around to the police. But I don't think we need do anything just yet.' They finished the wine and set off on a leisurely stroll in the direction of the harbour.

Fairy lights twinkled around the

wooden sign which read *The Lobster-pot Restaurant*, and reggae music filled the early evening air. It was the smells of spicy food wafting through the open doorway that enticed them inside.

'We'll try our luck and have something tasty for supper while we're here.' John smiled at his wife and ordered two of the house cocktails that were advertised on the board as having the ingredients of coconut, rum and fresh lemon with lime, a dash of vodka then topped up with brandy. Spicy chicken won from the menu choices.

'If it tastes as good as it smells, we'll be happy,' John said to the waiter as he placed the order.

It didn't take long for the young man with tied-back dreadlocks to deliver the drinks. Jean thanked him, then whispered to John, 'We'd better ask the questions before we drink these; otherwise we'll be talking double Dutch. Cheers, love, happy holidays.'

They touched glasses and John responded, 'Chin chin, bottoms up.' He took a swig and looked around for a likely target to question. 'Actually, there aren't so many people in here as there were in Fisherman's Creek the other night. Blast! We've come in to the wrong place.' He swivelled round; there were more holidaymakers than locals in this pub. 'Well, at least we've got a lovely drink and that spicy chicken really sold itself from the aroma.' He laughed and leaned back in his chair.

The young waiter was clearing glasses from a nearby table, and John accosted him.

'I bet you get to hear about all the happenings around here without even reading a paper, eh?'

Jean frowned. His line of enquiry needed a bit of polish, but at least he was asking.

'Yeah, mostly, there's not much we don't get to hear about.'

'What's new, then — anything?' John rocked back in his chair, his ears buzzing for some information. 'It's just that we made friends with this English journalist, who went off on a ferry boat, and we thought she'd have been back here by now. Not that we're worried or anything, just concerned a bit, that's all.'

'I need to check on your food. I'll ask in the kitchen, see if anyone has heard.' He sauntered up to the bar, and then looped round and through the double swing doors where the aroma of spicy food and delicious smells of fruit and fish wafted into the small, dimly-lit restaurant as he disappeared.

'I'd have gone into the subject gradually.' Jean sipped on her cocktail, and looked around, disappointed not to see any familiar faces from the hotel.

Just then Kathleen-Miranda Beckingsworth flounced up to the bar. She wafted her hand to order beer for the straight-laced man accompanying her and a gin and tonic for herself.

'Psst, don't look now.' Jean made enormous eyes and crouched across the table.

John immediately glanced around

and fixed his eyes on the latest arrival to the Lobster Pot.

'I said . . . Oh, never mind,' Jean huffed, then whispered, 'Act normal.' She sat up straight and gave her husband a huge smile.

'So, darling, what shall we do tomorrow?' John had taken the hint and was making small talk. 'We could take a ferry across to one of the smaller islands, what about that?'

Jean wanted to laugh, but nodded and kept the flashy woman at the bar in her side vision.

'Thing is, it's all mine by rights — or it would be, if he'd only do the decent thing and marry me.' Kathleen was no shrinking violet and wasn't aware that the elderly couple sitting at the table behind the door were listening in. 'All I want to do is get things straight in my mind. You understand where I'm coming from surely, Claude?'

'Naturally you want to be married to the father of your little girl.' The well-dressed gentleman evidently didn't want to upset her. 'I don't blame you wanting to get your hands on his assets. Who wouldn't?'

'Well, the lads will be back soon, hopefully and then I can set my little plan in action. And if he doesn't play ball, well, then I will have no other option, will I?'

'Not at all, dear, you go for it. Shall we eat here, or somewhere else?' They flicked through the menu, drinking rather quickly, Jean thought.

'You know, it's too quiet in here.' Kathleen flicked her hair back and scanned the room. 'Good for chatting though, but the food is better in the Fisherman's Creek, and the company.' She studied the man sitting opposite. 'It's good of you to fly out at such short notice, though — there aren't many solicitors who'd come half way around the world at such short notice, Claude.'

'I was due a break, and when you said you'd pay for my flight and hotel bill on Neptune, how could I resist?' Claude drained his beer.

'And there was me thinking it was my enchanting company you wanted.' She laughed.

'I think you've known me long enough to know you're barking up the wrong tree there,' Claude returned. 'But if we can get your estranged lover, the dashing Lord Broderick Loveday in hand — or should I say, Robinson Crusoe — then I'm all for a bit of an adventure.' He raised his eyebrows and sucked in his cheeks.

Jean peeked across at the couple by the bar and felt herself go warm. Her hands began to shake, and her breathing quickened. As they got up to leave she glanced at John, but waited silently until the couple had gone.

'Did you hear that?' she whispered hoarsely. 'Broderick Loveday . . . I'm sure that's the name Serena mentioned. He's the one she was looking for.'

'But it was monkeys she was after, if I recall?' John looked puzzled.

Giving a huge sigh, Jean closed her eyes. 'Yes, originally, but there was this chap she met on the flight over. Honestly, John, keep up . . . she said he was a bit of a recluse. Well, that flashy tart is after him! We need to find Serena and warn her to get back here pronto. And she didn't mention him being a Lord. Something smells really fishy around here, John — you know I'm never wrong.'

The waiter arrived with the meals and smiled.

'Enjoy your food — there's not much I can tell you about your friend, but they tell me the ferryman who took her to the remote island did say they'd met with the local bad boys on the way over. However she was safe and enjoying the hospitality of the locals over there.' He backed away and left them to their supper.

Jean picked at her chicken.

'Bad boys?' she kept interrupting her eating to mouth the words quietly in John's direction. 'I don't like the sound of this at all, John.' She frowned and ate another morsel. 'We need to get in touch with the police now. Something really wrong is going on around here.'

15

The evening had mellowed, and a soft, balmy breeze replaced the light shower of rain. Tangy scents of lemon and lime drifted from the trees which punctuated the walk along to the pub, Fisherman's Creek.

The bar was chock full to the rafters with locals, relaxing after work. This was one place not shown in any guide books or leaflets, yet most nights you could easily find more than half the customers were tourists. Fisherman's Creek was one of those drinking places that suited everyone.

Views across the bay in the early evening were reason enough for passers-by to linger, enjoy a glass of Fisherman's rum punch, and catch up with local gossip. Some of the ferrymen preferred a quiet beer down near the breakwater near where they left their boats for the night. John and Jean had realised this was the place they ought to have gone to first — but at least from that meal in the Lobsterpot, they knew they must take action now.

'I'll ask around the ferrymen and see if we can talk to Nicky,' Jean said, just before they entered the noisy packed bar.

'Did that fancy woman from the hotel remember us, do you think?' John really hoped not, but wasn't sure. 'She didn't seem the type to get too friendly, did she?'

'Thank goodness for that,' Jean retorted. 'She's not one I'd like to sit chatting to — too false by half. Too full of herself to even know we were there.'

'Let's try and keep it like that.' John pushed the door open and made his way into the bar.

'Totally agree with you, love.' Jean followed her husband into Fisherman's Creek.

'Can I have that in writing?' John

teased, then raised his eyebrows with his trademark smile and went to order them a drink.

★ ★ ★

Broderick laced his boots and supervised Shami and Rhawand, making sure they kept in his sight as they all trooped down the hill that felt more like a mountain to Serena. Her feet were aching and she really wanted to wash — preferably in the cool water of the lagoon, but on her own. Until she found out more about this map and treasure, and all the secrets that seemed to surround Broderick Loveday, she would keep her distance.

Agwe followed behind. Serena noticed he was keeping an eye towards the bay whenever she turned to check he was still there.

She longed to ask what the pirate ship was doing, and whether any of the Blackeye Wanderers might be coming ashore. Seeing as his wife, Cindy and daughter Sky-Blou along with his other children were at Broderick's camp, organising food, she couldn't imagine they would be. Surely Agwe wouldn't let his family sit there in the hollow by the beach if a dinghy full of pirates were likely to jump ashore.

Giving herself a mental shake, Serena took a couple of deep breaths. A tiny, opportunist voice in her head whispered, *This will make a great story when you get out of here.* She immediately blanked that thought and asked the question that was foremost in her mind.

'Broderick! You never did explain to Agwe what the treasure was . . . We'd all like to know, wouldn't we, boys?' Unsure where her nerve had come from, she made sure she spoke loud enough for everyone to hear. This silly game has gone on long enough. 'Was it diamonds, and is that why a ship full of pirates lies in wait over there?'

She pointed towards the ship; there was no mistaking the glint from the telescope that followed their direction.

'Get down, all of you.' Broderick pushed the two local lads to a sitting position, and the others followed suit, Chunky Monkey included. 'They're watching our every move — and they expect you two to deliver the goods?' He eyed the two boys suspiciously. 'And has he paid you upfront?'

'I'll bet they spoke to Danny Monsoon.' Agwe shot a sideways look at Broderick. Shami and Rhawand were silent. 'And he would have promised a wedge of cash, no doubt.' Agwe gave a sarcastic laugh and nodded. 'The bank of Danny Monsoon — no cash involved, of course. Don't tell me you didn't think he might send the lads after you, if he ever did pay up.' Agwe put his face near to Shami's frightened one. 'And now we're all being watched — and one thing I don't like is me and my loved ones being watched.' He looked away in disgust.

'We only wanted to earn a few dollars.' Shami looked from Broderick to Agwe, opening his palms as if begging them to understand. 'There was never going to be any funny business. It was this woman. She approached us on Neptune Island in a bar. She'd asked around, we heard — head-hunted us.'

'Don't tell me . . . ' Broderick sneered, then looked up to the sky. 'She'd be flashy,' he spoke slowly and deliberately, 'glamorous but not really all that pretty and wearing large sunglasses. Oh, and I imagine a wide-brimmed hat.' He held his hands a foot away from his head, indicating the size of her headgear, then waited for them to deny he was right. 'And skin covered in lashings of a really dark fake tan, more mahogany sideboard than anything else. Long fingernails, likely painted red.' Broderick halted for a breath. 'Am I close?'

The two boys looked at each other and Shami gave a brief nod. 'That does sound quite like the one we spoke to.'

'Aw, she's his ex, man — the woman

who wants him to get married and settle down. Can you tell he's still in love with her?' Agwe teased.

Serena's heart beat a little faster. This woman he described sounded like a proper celebrity — maybe an actress or model. Someone who would never look twice at Broderick, the rough-living island man; then she remembered him telling her about the life he wanted to forget back in London. He'd never mentioned a woman.

Why, when she didn't want him herself, should Serena suddenly feel threatened? As if she was losing her grip on what she wanted most. This was ridiculous; she *didn't* want him, and he was only a distraction while she'd been doing her research for Explorer Magazine.

'If nobody minds, I'm really tired and hungry. Did you say the food was ready?' She glanced at Broderick, determined not to let the thoughts of a woman on Neptune Island looking for him, or up to some trickery get to her.

'Can we go and eat? Would you say it's safe?' She looked towards Agwe, hoping for him to say yes.

'Well, I'm safe, and you're safe . . . ' Agwe took her hand. 'Don't worry too much about him either.' He nodded towards Broderick. 'He might be a poetry-reading recluse with a habit of talking to a monkey that appears and disappears like the Cheshire Cat, but he can look after himself, I know that for a fact. No English bounty hunter woman will ever tame him.'

'I'm sure you're right.' Serena walked on with Agwe, and was glad when she looked back to see the others following. The mystery of whatever Shami and Rhawand had been looking for was still unknown. She stopped in her tracks and swung round.

'There isn't any treasure — is there?'

He stood tall, those hypnotic eyes fixed on her for quite some time. It unsettled her but she matched his stare, waiting for an answer. When he spoke, he took a deep breath, and it was in a quiet and gentle voice.

'I have a property, quite a substantial one — not the two-up, two-down where I carelessly left this sketch of a map in a private drawer showing where I planned to hide the treasure.' The two boys hung on his every word. 'I keep the deeds to that property here on the island. A copy of it is also with my solicitor, back in London, so any attempts to steal this one would be futile.' He grinned at Shami and Rhawand who didn't know where to look. 'But if you like to play adventure games, that's fine by me. I quite like them myself.' He stole a glance in Serena's direction.

'The lady you spoke to is a head hunter; though I rather think it's my head she hunts as opposed to either of yours, I'm sorry to inform you.'

Serena could see now why he wanted to stay on the island out of the way of such a person. She also knew that in life it was fight or flight, and he was choosing the latter. She really needed to talk to him alone. She would make him see sense and not let some dominating woman bully him.

He was such a gentle character; she knew that. He really deserved to live his life without hiding away on some deserted island, overlooked by pirates, reading poems by moonlight. Though the thought of how intimate they had almost become earlier when he was quoting Byron by the fireside made her tremble with pleasure. She really had imagined they were the only man and woman in the world, and it both scared and excited her.

Agwe let out a cry. 'OK, folks, this just got serious, there's a rowing boat making its way over here. Let's go.' He took to the scrub path and shouted back to the others, 'You take the path, I need to take the scenic route.'

He plunged into the brambles and down a slope that didn't look safe to Serena's eyes. She looked to Broderick.

'We're right behind you.' He slung the monkey onto Serena's shoulders.

'Follow me — and you two,' he prodded Shami and Rhawand, 'make yourselves useful now.' He parted the pathway with the scythe he'd confiscated earlier, and then shouted to Agwe. 'Mate, catch . . . ' He twirled the other knife through the air. It somersaulted a couple of times before landing just near where Agwe was kicking and parting the scrub.

'You're both in charge of keeping Serena safe,' he rasped at the lads, and then glanced at her. His grey eyes were like charcoal burning deep, causing her stomach to lurch. 'That's an order.' He charged after his friend. 'Right behind you, Agwe; take it steady, it'll be a while before they're ashore.' He turned back to make sure Shami and Rhawand were one in front and one behind Serena, helping her on the steep slope. 'We're cutting as much scrub as we can, just be careful of pot holes.' Then he was gone.

16

We're worried about our friend.' John spoke quickly and with precision. He wanted to make sure the Detective Inspector on Neptune Island was absolutely clear about why they were raising the alarm.

'Of course we do realise she's a grown woman, yes. And she's got her own mind, but it was when Nicky the ferryman said they'd encountered some local pirate wannabes on the way over. You can't be too careful — and she'd spoken about coming on more trips with us. There's been neither sight nor sound of her since she left. We'd like you to check up if you could.'

Detective Inspector Roger Dean was the latest recruit in the police department on Neptune. In general he led a quiet life, and wasn't often needed to solve crime, other than a petty theft during tourist season, or a smuggling group. The latter was ongoing; he wondered if that one would ever get sorted.

Now he was faced with an elderly couple who were obviously taken with a fellow traveller. He could tell they wouldn't go away until he had thoroughly checked out where their friend was, and what she was doing. He offered them a chair each and asked them to start at the beginning and tell him all they knew.

The couple had asked around earlier in Fisherman's Creek, and after listening to what Nicky had told them, they knew they had to move fast. Luckily, DI Dean was still at work in his office in the back of the local police station.

'We got a taxi over here as soon as we heard you work late most nights,' Jean explained. 'We're so glad you were still here. We'd become quite close to Serena, and she didn't plan to stay away long — I'm sure about that.'

She watched as the forms began to

pile up. Writing things down as he listened, looking up occasionally, the inspector finally had all the information he needed. Over an hour later, he reassured them both that he would do all he could to find Serena and let her know they were concerned about her.

'At least if we know she's all right — that's the main thing we want to know,' Jean reiterated.

DI Dean nodded reassuringly and went the extra mile by dropping a somewhat happier John and Jean back at their hotel in his Jeep.

★   ★   ★

'It's awfully steep, and I'm not wearing the best shoes for this.' Serena tripped her way down the hillside like a little pony. 'I'm frightened I might fall.' She hated to be a whinge, but the thought of going head over heels overwhelmed her. 'Can I sit down for a minute?'

Once she'd had a little break, she held her hand to her head and took some deep breaths, glad that Shami and Rhawand stayed with her.

'I carry a bottle of rum if you want a swig.' Shami produced a small bottle from his jacket pocket. 'It's all right; it's neat, not got anything else mixed with it.'

'What — you carry alcohol around with you? Even when you're steering the ferry boat?'

If Serena hadn't been so afraid she wouldn't have taken a taste, but she was glad to feel the fiery drink slipping down her throat.

'Thanks — that's made me feel better.' She handed it back. 'I must admit, I'm glad you had it.' She didn't really want to approve of the young man carrying drink, but nothing surprised her any more around here.

'We'd be better to keep moving, and then we can see what's going on down there.' The young lad nodded in the direction Broderick and Agwe had disappeared in a while ago.

Shami and Rhawand offered a hand

to hoist Serena up. She let out a slow breath and began the downhill trek again. When the lads kept hold of her hands, she didn't object. Just when she was gaining confidence, she lost her footing and slipped, almost landing on her behind. 'Oh my word, I don't think I'm cut out for this . . . ' She bit her lip trying not to show her discomfort.

'Right; only one thing for it.' Rhawand nodded to his friend and crossed his forearms.

'What! Is that a sign of the pirates or what?'

'No, it's how we make a chair.' The boys linked hands, scooped her up to sit on their arms and made swift work navigating the slippery slopes.

Serena clung on, her arms looped around both their necks. She half screamed and then laughed as she was whisked down the mountain like the queen of the jungle.

'Oh, Broderick will never believe you've had to carry me. He'll call me a proper townie.'

'Better than how you were trying to do it.' The boys grinned at each other as they neared the end of the journey and set her down gently. Broderick, standing in the clearing, witnessed her safe landing.

'Well, glad to see chivalry is still alive on the island.' He patted the two lads on the back, and looked Serena up and down, as if checking she was all in one piece. 'It's a tricky route, but the quickest. You could have gone the longer way and been safer.'

Serena shook her head. 'I wouldn't want to be too far behind you.'

'Is that us forgiven?' Shami's eyes were huge and he looked sheepish.

Broderick patted his pocket that contained the papers but didn't reply.

'How's Agwe? Are his family all right?' Serena looked over towards the ocean, and towards the camp. Delicious aromas drifted over the trees.

'Come and see for yourself.' He led her through the trees, to where Agwe wrestled on the ground with a man twice his size. As she gasped, Broderick's best mate had the stranger in an arm lock and then dragged him the length of the clearing. Serena guessed this man was a pirate.

'Oh, no! I hope nobody's going to get badly hurt.' Serena wanted to run, but stood beside Broderick clasping his hand.

He leaned towards her and whispered. 'Agwe likes to offer unwelcome visitors a little rum punch on arrival to make sure they know who's in charge.' He smiled and immediately Serena relaxed. 'They like to project a hard image, but once they've had some rum and good food, they're not so bad. That's not to say they ride on the right side of the law, though. The police will catch up with them one of these days.'

In no time, the gabble of friendly chatter and laughter could be heard. An old ruffian with a necktie and a gold tooth at the front of his mouth was using a piece of bread to scoop food from a bowl. He slapped his knee and roared with laughter as Agwe was relating the story of how the two wannabe pirates got soaked in the waterfall and were caught unawares from above. Chunky the monkey danced in front of the crowd, chattering and eating any fruit he could get hold of while the children played with the other seafarer with the parrot on his shoulder.

'He can repeat anything you tell him — watch this.' The old pirate leaned his head round. 'Give us a kiss, missus, give us a kiss.' He gave a cheeky grin in Cindy's direction, then winked at Agwe. The parrot copied every word and the group of friends shrieked. That set the children off with a string of naughty words and Cindy had to intervene.

Serena watched with amusement. The men were obviously well lubricated with rum, and so far there didn't seem to be any trouble, but she was wary of what might occur next.

Broderick led her to the side and

whispered in her ear. 'We need to talk before you leave the island.'

She nodded. 'I'd like that.'

He pushed one of her braids behind her shoulder. 'This hairstyle was a good move, and it suits you.' He smiled.

'Thanks. And they haven't robbed you for the deeds to your property.' Serena wanted to ask about the lady who was after his private property, and if she'd been in his house to get the map, did he live with her? But for now she didn't feel the time was right.

'Come here.' He reached for her hand and pulled her to sit next to him on the log which made a comfortable bench. 'What happens next for you?' He looked deep into her eyes.

'Well, I have to get on with my work. But I've had a brilliant idea.' Serena bubbled inside; why hadn't she thought of it before? 'You are to be the main subject of my articles. In fact . . .' She turned towards the man she'd been so close to for most of the time she'd been in the Caribbean.

'You are living the life so many people only dream of, but would never dare try. And since knowing you, I have seen lots of sides to your personality. Imagine; there are pictures on my camera of you with Chunky on your shoulders. The way you strode up the mountain there.' She glanced up towards the lagoon where the suspense had nearly frightened her senseless.

'And you know real life pirates, and they're over there eating your jambalaya. It'd be such a scoop; can I have your permission to do that?' She didn't wait for him to reply, how could he refuse her when it would make him into a household name? 'Sales of the magazine will rocket, and I wouldn't be surprised if they want lots more stories on you, or even a diary. You'd be able to come back to London and be free of the woman that is keeping you away from your homeland.'

Raving about her latest plan, Serena hadn't noticed the way Broderick had stiffened and gone quiet. She was so wrapped up in her big idea she hadn't noticed that he had let go of her hand and inched away from her. It was only when he spoke she knew exactly what he thought of her plan.

'If you think that is a good idea, then you don't know me at all.' She reached for his hand and tried to look him in the eye, but he'd completely shut down. 'Get away from me, Serena. Don't try and speak to me ever again.'

He turned to face her for one short moment, and when he did she saw a man she didn't recognise. But then she did. It was the same cold, hard stranger she'd sat next to on the plane journey. He looked gaunt, distant and completely alone. Not the Broderick she'd grown to know and . . . and . . .

Her heart sank. *How did I get it so wrong?*

'There will be plenty of ferry boats going back across to Neptune in the morning — or by the looks of it, even sooner than that.'

A police speedboat screamed across

the bay and floodlights swept the beach as a megaphone blasted out a request.

'Serena Winter, requesting news of Serena Winter — anybody of that name, or anyone who knows of her, please make yourself known.'

When Serena moved to tell the others she would go to the beach and talk to the police, no one was to be seen. All she saw was the smouldering fire and a pot emptied of jambalaya. When she turned round, Broderick was gone, as well as the others. Did she imagine them all, or was she going crazy?

Either way, she was glad to walk along the soft sand and be hauled aboard the boat that would take her back to Neptune. As the police boat made a U-turn and headed across the water, she saw the Ruby Queen lurking in the mist.

So I didn't imagine them.

If that was his attitude, she could live without Broderick Bloody Loveday, Mr Mystery — or more likely, he was delusional. Time to get on with the job she came here to do — and at least she did have some great photos to be going on with.

From now on, it would be a more civilised Serena exploring the Caribbean islands.

The trouble was, though she hardly dare admit it — she was missing him a little bit already.

17

It was a tired and emotional Serena who debarked from the police rescue boat in Neptune harbour. She promised to go down to the police station as soon as she'd been back to her lodgings to wash, change and get some rest.

She was pleased that DI Roger Dean had only asked a couple of questions.

'Have you been held captive?'

'No.'

'Did you stay over on the island of your own free will at all times?'

'Yes, I did some exploring and research for my work,' she had explained. Apart from that he'd not said much more, other than to say he had men who were searching the island.

Only when they neared the harbour he'd told her that he'd need to take a statement later in the day if she could pop by. 'You have good friends at your hotel.' He smiled. 'They were concerned. You need to go and see them as soon as you can to put their minds at rest.'

Serena knew immediately it must be John and Jean. She looked forward to seeing them and telling them about her adventures — but some bits she'd keep to herself.

'I really need to drop off at my lodgings, but I promise to talk to them first thing.'

Serena yawned and felt as if her legs had turned to lead. When the DI told her he'd already sent word to let her friends know she was safe, Serena sighed and nodded her thanks.

★ ★ ★

It felt like an age since she'd been in Ackee Grove Cottage, and it didn't hold the magic that she'd imagined when she'd climbed aboard the plane on her adventure of a lifetime. But then she didn't know of secluded islands, where wonderful wild herbs grew and cool mountain-top lagoons awaited. She pushed all thoughts of the rugged island man away. He was akin to one of those annoying tunes that kept popping into your head. *I know a man who gets on my nerves, gets on my nerves* . . . She smiled despite herself. It was an odd feeling, knowing she'd never see him again.

Pedro and Maria had welcomed her when she pushed open the door and flopped down onto a rattan chair; they didn't question her other than to say, 'It's the effect the Caribbean has on most English tourists. You'll get drawn in to the lifestyle and won't ever want to go back home.'

Serena frowned, and pulled her braids into a bunch behind her head.

'I'm not sure about that . . . What I would like is a hot bath and a good sleep, and then I have work to do.'

Once she had washed and changed into a cool caftan that Maria had draped across her bedside table, Serena flopped down on her comfortable bed and sighed, 'Ahh, such luxury.'

When she snuggled between the sheets, just before that much-needed sleep finally came, she couldn't help feeling something was missing. Of course, she realised — the sound of waves lapping the shore. That's what she missed, and if she listened hard enough, she could swear she heard a distant cry of dolphins. In her dreams they swam in loops around her while monkeys chattered and smiled their silly smiles.

When she woke, Serena struggled for a moment to remember where she was. It was the smell from the coffee machine and the lilt of Maria's gentle singing that prised her from the comfort of the huge, low-lying bed. From the side window, she watched Pedro tending the garden.

She dressed quickly in a checked blouse and crisp white shorts, making sure she had notebook, pens and laptop at the ready.

When she logged on, she had a Wi-Fi connection, so quickly she dashed an email off to Rita Parker, her editor in the UK.

It's all right, I'm still alive, been across to one of the smaller islands. Lots to report, and sending copy and photographs later today. Serena Winter.

Immediately a message pinged into her inbox.

Good — we were starting to wonder — about to send out a search party. Any monkeys yet?

Rita Parker — Features Editor, Explorer Magazine

Yes, will be in touch ASAP. Regards, Serena Winter Roving reporter

Later, over a delicious breakfast, cooked by Maria, and several cups of coffee, Serena discovered that the Ju Ju man could be found on the island of Kiri-kiri and the ferry left every hour.

'Your cookery will have me weighing a stone heavier by time I come to leave,' Serena laughed.

'Not with all the walking and exploring you've been telling us about this morning.'

Maria and Pedro waved her off and as she closed the gate. Serena had already made her mind up that she would go and find the Ju Ju man — and somehow she thought calling him that would be better than asking John and Jean if they wanted to visit the Witch Doctor.

She smiled as she made her way along to the Atlantis Hotel to see her friends. It was all in fun, and there wasn't anything he could tell her that she didn't already know anyway.

18

Serena couldn't resist a stroll along the harbour before meeting up with John and Jean. She guessed they'd still be relaxing and doing their usual morning crossword for a while yet.

As she rounded the corner where row upon row of boats waited for likely passengers, a flashing light from a stationary police van caught her eye. Among the commotion two young lads were bundled from a boat and into the back of the vehicle — pulled by the scruff of their necks. There was no mistaking the pair of ragamuffins — they'd only recently helped her down the mountainside over on the Island of Shells. Shami and Rhawand; she could only stand and stare as they were driven away.

They must have been taken in for questioning, yet why? They didn't steal anything. Broderick would never press charges.

Then again, how would I have any clue about what he'd do? He's only a stranger I met on a plane.

Serena covered her mouth with her hand. There must be some mistake . . . Should she go down to the police station? Why wasn't Broderick with them? Not for one minute that she wanted to see or hear from him. But surely if anyone was to blame for them searching for his map, it had to be the person who sent them on the trail. And from what she'd heard, that woman was staying in the Atlantis Hotel.

Then she remembered the statement she had to make and knew she'd have to pop along, even though she didn't want to get any more deeply involved than she already was.

* * *

Making the necessary comments and telling everything she knew about

280

Shami and Rhawand didn't take as long as she thought. The youths were being held a bit longer to answer more questions relating to drug smuggling.

After she walked back to the harbour front, Serena remembered her other plans for the morning. She glanced up the road towards the rock face, where the magnificent Atlantis Hotel jutted out from the hill giving residents the most stunning views out to sea.

Shielding her eyes from the morning sun, she saw someone waving from the long conservatory. The figure of a woman emerged onto the wooden balcony. Jean shouted over.

'Serena! It's great to see you. Come on up.'

With a smile as wide as her face, Serena gave an exaggerated wave back to Jean and nodded. A few long strides, then half a run and she'd quickly reached the top. It wasn't long before she received the warmest of welcomes from the couple she'd come to know and love in such a short space of time.

'We were worried.' John pushed his puzzle book to one side and stood to greet her as she sat down with them. He ordered coffee and Jean told him not to forget those exquisite Caribbean pastries filled with exotic fruits and drizzled with icing.

The model-like woman moved with panache as she passed their table. She made her way through the conservatory, only giving them a sidelong glance. Then she turned back.

'Haven't we met before? I'm sorry but we seem to miss each other at breakfast.' She gave an exaggerated giggle. 'Either I'm early or you're late or vice versa. I didn't know your daughter was staying with you?' She stood waiting for them to reply.

'I'm a friend, but not staying here, I'm afraid.' Serena spoke first. 'Well I did stay a day or so, but that was before . . . ' She stopped herself from saying any more to the stranger — and she didn't want to remember any kindness from him.

282

Could this be that Kathleen person who wants to get her claws into my Broderick — argh! — that Broderick?

'We're usually engrossed in our papers, that's probably what it is. And you're here on holiday yourself, then?' Jean enquired.

'Mmm, kind of on a mission, but sometimes it seems like an impossible one. If only men knew what was good for them, life would be simpler, don't you think?' She pulled on a large, floppy hat over her glossy hair and gave a swish of her flowing cardigan, and then she was gone.

Serena gaped and turned to Jean.

'She's the one he spoke about — has to be.' Her shoulders tensed. 'It's her fault those two lads are being held in the police station — and she's after Broderick's money.'

'You need to tell someone all you know, love. Have you spoken to the police?' Jean pulled up her chair. 'And there's something else you really need to know . . . '

★ ★ ★

The threesome stood in the queue waiting for the ferry to Kiri-Kiri. It hadn't taken much persuading from Serena for the couple to go with her to visit the Ju Ju man.

'And you say he was nothing like a lord at all?' Jean had listened to all the details about Serena's visit to the Island of Shells, but she couldn't help but wonder if Serena had left some bits out. The girl seemed different since she'd been over there — more grown up and a lot quieter.

'She's here, that Miranda woman, and up to no good.' Jean tutted as she continued. 'We heard her talking to that other flash Harry chap she has staying with her. Trying to trap her ex or something, but if he's not interested in her why is she bothering? Some people never know when to take no for an answer, do they?'

'I think she's made that part up.' Serena gave a puzzled frown. 'He's more like a tramp than a lord. Really, he's not like that at all. He's more like . . . ' She scrunched her face up and then wondered why she was bothering to talk and think about such a rude, moody person. 'Who cares? Let's enjoy the day trip, shall we? Look, they've begun boarding now. And from now on, after today, I'll have to be working, so excuse me if I'm taking pictures and on the laptop a lot. With island hopping and spending time doing fun things like swimming with dolphins, and climbing mountains . . . ' Words got stuck in her throat as she had a vision of a perfect male bathing under the waterfall. *NO! He's not perfect not even close to it; he's yucky, dirty, and messy. Oh, I miss him.*

Her heart skipped a beat. The ache inside almost made her sick. Quickly she sneaked a look in the direction of his island, hoping to see a smoke signal or something to show he was still there. Not a sign.

Who cares? Forget him, Serena, he's

nothing to you. A passing stranger that lent you a hammock for the night. Let that Miranda woman have him, she's welcome, and in fact they suit each other, the pair of oddballs.

Her stomach lurched at the thought of anyone else getting close to him. He wasn't the kind of man to make friends easily, she knew that.

I wonder if he misses me.

Jean was nudging her. They were approaching Kiri-Kiri, and all she'd done was daydream about someone she was trying hard to forget.

Focus, Serena; come on, get a grip.

'We're here, Serena. Look — there's a band to welcome us onto the island.'

A brass band was playing some familiar tunes and for a moment Serena wondered if she'd taken a detour and landed in Yorkshire. As the sun rose higher in the sky, and palm trees stood tall, wavering softly in the gentle breeze, the smell of charcoal and barbecued food filled the air.

Children danced wearing colourful

dresses, shorts and shirts. The sights and sounds were truly heart-warming and for the first time since she'd left Robinson Crusoe's island, she was completely distracted.

'Welcome to Kiri-Kiri.' A young lady pressed bunches of flowers into their arms, and gave them pieces of chopped fruit in a small bowl. The route from the jetty to the square where all the activity was taking place was strewn with flower petals. A boy grabbed handfuls from a bucket and made sure they walked over a pot-pourri carpet on arrival.

Over delicious coffee and more fruit, Serena noticed a local man watching them from the next table. She returned his smile and asked where they might find the Ju Ju man who, she'd heard, was the best in the Caribbean.

He smiled, revealing beautiful white teeth. Then speaking in that rhythmic tropical lilt, he said, 'Our Ju Ju lives in the middle of the island.' He nodded across the courtyard. 'You take the left-hand lane out of town and go down a track marked Kiri Cove. If the sea is out, you cross the causeway over the broken dam — and don't look down because there is a deep, dark snake pit.'

Serena was thinking she wasn't all that fussed about seeing this Ju Ju really.

'After that, you take the crocodile stepping stone walk over the estuary and beyond that there's a mountain where you'll find a gap in the wall. Then, deep, deep in the cave of mysterious happenings you will find him with his crystal ball and smoking his pipe of peace.'

Serena licked her top lip that tasted salty where she had broken into a mild sweat.

'Not sure about you two, but I wasn't over-keen on seeing him, what do you think?'

Their guide on the next table broke into a grin.

'But lucky for you, it's Thursday. He's always on his market stall when it's a full moon.'

He winked at Serena and got up and left.

She stared after him and pulled a face when he turned and gave her a jolly wave.

'Why, the . . . so-and-so was having me on.' She burst out laughing then finished her coffee.

'Maybe I will have a look at that market stall. Are you coming?' She stood and gathered her things while John and Jean were deciding whether to have another drink.

'You go on, love; John's just told me he's heard there's an old pirate ship over the other side of the island. We might go and see that first. And when you tell me how it went, then I might have a chat with the Ju Ju man — but you go, have fun. We could meet back her in a couple of hours.'

Serena gave them a wave, then followed the general direction in which groups of people were walking. The heat was almost too much and she now knew why Miranda wore such an oversized hat. The first thing she bought from the market was a sun hat, followed by sunglasses.

Hoping the scent of patchouli and jasmine was a clue, she followed the exotic aromas between the stalls and right to the end of the row; she spied a small gazebo with colourful feathers and beaded curtains hanging over the doorway tucked away in the corner among the stalls.

Bingo. It's the local Witch Doctor.

Any butterflies she may have had were more from excitement than fear. Glad to be seeing him in the local market place and not in the cave of mysterious happenings or whatever that chappie was telling her, she looked over the stall, wondering whether to buy some angel cards or a bag of runes. Unsure what she'd do with them, she waited.

A large man wearing a headdress of colourful feathers and more war paint than in the Westerns she used to watch on television appeared.

'You're looking for love?' He gazed deep into her eyes and began to hum a tune.

Typical sales chat for the tourist. As if!

'No — I'm a career woman, here with my work. I have a job to do. Just curious, that's all.'

Serena had a funny sensation as she looked into his deep, brown eyes. She blinked, went to leave, then made a rash decision.

'I'd like a consultation — reading. How does it work?' It was all for research, she reasoned.

'My name is Mr Martini Darjeelee, and a reading is only the price of decent cup of coffee, nothing more. Of course if you choose to buy from my stall, then that's perfectly fine by me.'

He led her into the tent and gestured for her to sit down. Wind chimes jangled and joss sticks filled the air with their musky scent. He asked her to hold out her hands, palms upwards. Then he took her hands and studied them for a while.

The shell ornaments dotted all around were really special. Serena had already decided she'd buy some of those as presents for her mum and dad. She glanced at Mr Martini Darjeelee, who had his eyes closed and was swaying gently.

'You are in love, but all is not as it should be.' He opened his eyes and looked directly at her.

She went to contradict him but he shushed her.

'No, you cannot see it, but the love of your life is waiting. A handsome man, who makes your heart beat, is coming over water.'

Serena stifled a giggle, not having the heart to tell him they were on an island, everyone has to come over water and she knew of no handsome men. Well, no, of course she didn't; he was wrong.

'You are going to settle down, but first comes the heartache, and the tempest will rise and then fall . . . Until one day, you will find your paradise and never look back. And you heard it here first.'

What a load of old bunkum, she wanted to tell him, but something stopped her. It was nearly Christmas — and it was nice to think she had some handsome stranger to look forward to, even if it was all make-believe.

She left with a bag full of shells and a special little pouch he'd assembled especially for her. He told her it contained a tiny shell, a pebble and a feather along with some herbs and spices. The Ju Ju bag had only cost ten dollars extra. The shells and other presents she'd purchased for her mum and dad had been a touch expensive, but having the reading was a good experience.

As he placed it around her neck, he chanted. 'There are a million stars in the sky, a thousand rocks on the beach, hundreds of people the whole world over but only one love for you.' He smiled and said, 'Take care.'

Serena left feeling happy; she guessed that was the magic of the Ju Ju. She couldn't wait to meet up with John and Jean, who were still gushing over the pirate ship adventure when she bumped into them in the square.

'It's well worth a look. They say it was really involved in smuggling years ago. The Ruby Queen is something to marvel at — honestly, Serena, it is.' John beamed.

Serena almost said there was a chance it still was used, but held her tongue. Her friends were so full of enthusiasm they'd almost forgotten to enquire about her adventure.

'He told me I'd find love in the Caribbean, which of course is a load of rot.' Serena scoffed. 'You'd do well to go and meet him, it's only over there.' She fingered her Ju Ju bag and watched in amazement as a tiny creature jumped onto the table next to where they were sitting. He'd grabbed a glass of wine and guzzled down the dregs in a trice.

'Drunken monkeys! At last, I've seen one!' Serena snapped away with her camera.

Once the monkey had swung away into the trees, they walked the length of the red dusty road until they came upon a traditional-looking hotel offering afternoon tea by the pool. Serena almost fainted with the delight of it all. The Jewel in the Crown really did live up to its name.

The threesome enjoyed a relaxing afternoon. Serena ordered tea and cakes and, still wearing the Ju Ju pouch, she opened up her laptop.

For the first time since she'd arrived in the Caribbean, she really got down to work. It was as if the monkey encounter had dispatched her writer's block. Nevertheless, she surprised herself when she told her friends she'd decided to stay on Kiri-Kiri for a few days. Everything was here for her to really get on and do the job she'd been sent to do, she explained enthusiastically.

Reluctantly, John and Jean waved goodbye and told her to keep in touch.

She told them she would, and then ordered more tea.

19

Tea on the terrace by the pool made her feel completely at home, and a steady band of monkeys hopped over the hedge and kept Serena entertained for the next couple of hours. With good Wi-Fi service she dashed another email off to Rita Parker, and crossed her fingers as she pressed send. She'd already let Pedro and Maria know that she wouldn't be back.

Decided to be right in the heart of the action, a lovely little place called Jewel in the Crown, and it really is. Would it be all right if I check in here for a few days to get a live diary going on the drunken monkeys? I have told the Ackee Grove people.

Regards, Serena W, roving reporter.

She hadn't heard back from Maria and Pedro, but she didn't imagine they'd check emails until the next day.

Either way, she'd booked in and decided she would stay here even if she had to pay for it herself.

There was no reply from Rita either, then she remembered the time difference. She'd have to wait until the next day to hear from her editor.

Luckily for Serena it was good news when she got the return email the following morning.

We can allow you a few days, as Ackee Grove agreed flexible terms. Make it worth our while. Send as much as you can, and we'll do a diary column on the monkeys as well as any other interesting articles.

Regards, Rita Parker

Features Editor for Explorer Magazine.

P.S. How's Robinson Crusoe? Photos?

Serena laughed out loud at the postscript, then gave a modest reply and decided to go for a swim before breakfast. Glad to make use of her bikini collection, she wore the floral one with a flattering cut that showed off her

Caribbean tan. Making her way to the dining area, she tied on a strapless sundress.

She helped herself to croissants with mango jam from the buffet bar and chose pineapple yogurt with chopped apple and nuts to go with it. Feeling slightly rude not to be taking the fresh Blue Mountain coffee of which the locals were so proud, she opted for breakfast tea; a large pot full so she'd be able to have more than one cup.

The difference with Jewel in the Crown was that she kept a low profile and nobody bothered her, as mostly she had her nose fixed firmly to her laptop. When she wasn't typing and sending articles, she lay back and topped up her tan. She hadn't been one for sunbathing back in England, but her limbs had turned the colour of honey and tiny freckles dotted her cheekbones.

When she flicked through her camera roll, she had to smile at some of the photos, and wondered if Kathleen-Miranda had swum across to the Island of Shells yet. For a man who wanted to escape the clutches of a woman possessed, Broderick hadn't done a very good job of it.

Glad to be out of the drama, Serena closed her laptop and took a walk. Her days had fallen into a regular routine, and she really wished she could stay longer, but Christmas in the Caribbean would be another experience she'd be able to write home about and it was only days away now. Her fingers flicked like lightning across her keyboard.

It was mid-afternoon; she'd taken a half-hour break and enjoyed a refreshing swim. Sun caused the water to glisten on her arms as she sat, head bent over the page, using pen and paper as a break from the computer screen.

A shadow fell across her notebook. Shielding her eyes from the sun, Serena looked up. The dark-haired stranger's grey eyes looked deep into hers. He didn't speak; she knew him. Now there was no mistaking the intense desire as he watched her. His toned and bronzed body was showing beneath his crisp white shirt — just enough for her to drop what she was doing and sit up straight.

He looks exactly like that man from the article in the newspaper. Lord Loveday —

'Broderick. It's you . . . '

Serena almost choked and words wouldn't come. Her breathing became rapid and she was aware of her bikini revealing more than she wanted in front of him. She was supposed to be alone, relaxing and getting on with her work, by the pool with nobody around. And now, here in front of her stood a vision of pure loveliness and she was struck senseless.

'Is that you, or could it be you're related to someone I know?' Serena babbled. It made her sound silly, but not half as silly as her mouth felt wobbling. If she didn't get in control of it soon, this vision of an alpha male would think he'd stumbled upon a complete and utter nutcase.

'You forget quickly.' He spoke slowly and kept his eyes on hers. 'Then again,' he bit on his lower lip and shyly gave the briefest of smiles. 'I might have let myself go a little bit.'

When he grinned, back was the man she'd spent time with on the Island of Shells.

'What happened? Your beard? And you've had a haircut and . . . ' She was getting too personal, but dark hair had replaced the frizzy grey mop. If she'd thought he was a bit of all right before, now he was an absolute dish. She had to know, but felt uneasy. Perhaps he wanted reassurance she wouldn't use any photographs — but she really wanted to send a photo of him to Rita, right away.

'I looked in the mirror one day. As you know, I don't make a habit of it.' He crouched down to be level with her and those grey eyes made her long to pull him close. He ran a finger gently along her cheek. 'It occurred to me that I'd met someone who made me feel happier than I have done for a long time. I stupidly let her go — but there's someone I want you to know about.'

Serena's heart pounded. *He's come to find me to say he's going back with Kathleen-Miranda. Just when I've met someone special. Great!*

'You told me — I've met her. Kathleen-Miranda was staying at the Atlantis Hotel, the one you kindly booked me into when I arrived, just after I thought that old shack was to be my lodgings.' She tried to keep a straight face but when their eyes met they both had to chuckle at the memory of the stinky old outhouse at the bottom of the garden at Ackee Grove.

Broderick's body slumped and he let out a sigh. 'Of course not Kathleen-Miranda, you know how she irritates the hell out of me. But there's someone else — she means the world to me.'

'So why are you here? What made you come and find me, all dapper with your new city slicker look?' She turned away, not wanting him to see her disappointment and then looked back sulkily. 'If there's someone else, what do you want from me?'

'I have a daughter. A little girl called Aileen.'

20

Aileen . . . and her mother is Kathleen-Miranda?' Why else would she be so persistent? Of course, it all made sense now. 'She's looking for you to pay maintenance, be a part of your daughter's life?' Serena wanted to ask so many questions yet forced herself to stay calm.

Broderick looked down and bit his lip. 'I give Kathleen a generous allowance for our daughter.' He looked up. 'Trouble is, it's never enough. She wants a ring, and my surname, a grand mansion, it never ends. It's turned out hideously, more of a nightmare; which is why I escape to the island whenever I can. Sometimes it's easier for Aileen if I keep out of the way.'

'Why did you come to find me?' Serena was all for keeping families together. 'If I'd known you were so involved I'd never have . . . '

It wasn't as if anything had happened so far but it had crossed her mind a time or two, nevertheless.

He gave a deep laugh. 'Do you really have to ask? Please tell me you've thought about me at least once or twice since you left?' He looked directly at her; it was time to be honest.

'I'm not a home-wrecker, and if there's any chance of you and her — ' The words almost got stuck in her throat. 'How often do you see Aileen? Surely you must miss spending time with her?'

This was torture. Serena's head was saying, *tell him to go back, anywhere but not here standing in front of me looking good enough to eat.* Her heart wanted to reach out and hold him tight and never let him go.

'There's no home to wreck. I only get to see Aileen when it suits Kathleen. My daughter is a pawn in the game of 'Kathleen gets what Kathleen wants' only she'll never wear my ring, or live with me or what she wants most, parade with a fancy title. She'll get nothing whatsoever from me.' His jaw stiffened and the smouldering grey eyes had turned to steel. 'It happened in a moment of madness, but there are no regrets when I see that little girl smile.'

Part of her wanted to be pleased, but knowing there was an innocent little child in the midst of all the bitterness only made Serena feel sad. Especially when it was clear how much he loved the little mite.

'I'm sorry about the situation, you should have told me sooner.' Would she have fallen in so deep if she'd known he was Daddy to a toddler?

'Can I tell you the real reason why I came, apart from being honest and telling you about the love of my life?' He moved until he was inches away from her. 'I recently found the woman who makes me feel alive, and gives me hope for the future. Only trouble is, it's been so long since anyone had this effect on me . . . ' He gently pressed his lips to hers and Serena almost swooned from sheer delight as she returned his kiss.

'Shall we order champagne?'

Broderick kept his eyes on her, and trying hard not to break into a silly grin, Serena nodded.

'That's a good idea, but I'm a tea drinker by day, and they do a lovely strong cuppa. We could share a pot.' She didn't want to give in and say yes to everything he said; besides, champagne would go straight to her head, though she was tempted. 'I need to freshen up — if I'd known you were going to show up . . .'

'I'll arrange for the tea to be sent up to your suite, while you make yourself comfortable. Did I say I've booked the room opposite yours?' Broderick flashed a smile, and strode away towards the hotel kitchen to organise refreshments.

Serena took several deep breaths to calm the thump in her heart. Yet it felt so right, talking, getting to know each other more . . . and being with him was easy.

★ ★ ★

Back in her room, Serena quickly showered and sprayed cologne, then changed into her white cotton shorts and loose pink T-shirt. Nothing she did could calm the butterflies having a party inside her.

Broderick knocked on her door, entered when she called out and sat down on the easy chair by her window. She listened while he told her more about Aileen and how he had made provisions for her schooling and anything else she might need.

'Spending time with you is what your daughter really needs, rather than just things you've provided.' Serena kept a distance, not letting herself fall into his arms as she yearned to do, and keeping the conversation on his daughter rather than in the moment for fear of making a fool of herself.

'I wanted you to know about Aileen, it's important to me, but as I said, that's not my only reason for coming to find you — '

The knock on the door, and a call of 'Room service,' halted his speech. Along with the afternoon tea, a bucket of champagne on ice was delivered to her room. Broderick had also ordered lobster salad for them both and fruit for afters.

Serena had only just begun to pour the tea when Broderick took her hand.

'Serena; leave that, come here. I've wanted to do this since you walked into my life.'

He pulled her close and held her so tight she could feel his heart pounding against her chest. Was he shaking? Or maybe it was she who trembled at the feel of his warm body against hers. Every bit of her fitted exactly into him as if they were two parts of a jigsaw puzzle just made for each other.

When he let her go and stepped back, it was to study her face then gently press his lips to hers once again. Serena kissed him properly, forgetting everything else apart from being here with this man; the one she'd only recently met, but knew in her heart she wanted to be with. His tongue was tickling hers and she moaned with pleasure, almost in heaven when she felt his hands holding her close underneath her top.

His shirt was open and after nuzzling into him, tasting the gorgeousness of his body, she tugged it off over his head and grabbed his firm shoulders. Any ideas they might have had about eating salad were gone. Serena could only act on instinct, and right now her instincts were telling her to lie down and pull him onto the bed with her.

Next minute he was lifting her onto the bed proving he felt the same. Quickly they undressed each other, and kissed and caressed until they mingled as one. The feel of his strong hands finding all the right places and his gentle kisses all over sent a tingle of pleasure through her whole being. She wanted him, and knew this was the moment, the way he kissed her more urgently.

More than an hour later, completely fulfilled, they finally fell asleep entwined in each other's arms. Eventually, hungry from their rapturous lovemaking, they woke and remembered the lobster salad.

Broderick fed Serena olives from his plate, and she pierced a chunk of juicy tomato and placed it delicately in his mouth, all the time wanting to kiss him again.

Over the meal, Broderick explained what happened after Serena had left the Island of Shells.

'I took a ferry over to Neptune and paid a visit to the police station. Shami and Rhawand have been released without charge. Nothing was taken; I explained they were acting on a fool's errand.' Broderick ran a tanned hand through his new hairstyle and the dark curls bounced back into place. 'I called into a spa, as you've noticed.'

Serena wondered how much he'd paid for the makeover. 'You spoke to Kathleen?'

'I had to call in to the Atlantis, and yes, of course I did. She was there with that silly lawyer of hers, and I told her there's no chance of any reunion. Not that there was any union to start with, well, other than . . . '

'I don't want details. Were John and Jean there? They're my friends who warned me about Kathleen — she was going to send someone after you. It was them who went to the police.'

Serena noticed how his newly styled hair was already looking wilder than it had when he'd first turned up. More like her Broderick on his castaway island. Making love suited him; he needed to do it again . . . soon.

He smiled. 'They were, and they kindly told me where I might find you. They're a friendly couple.'

Serena nodded. 'It must be lovely to be so comfortable with someone you've known almost all your life.' She blushed as she noticed him looking at her once again with such intensity it almost took her breath away. 'They went to look round the Ruby Queen — a pirate ship from years ago, like a museum, John told me. It's anchored on Kiri-Kiri. They're doing a good trade according to my friends, and spreading the word on local history.'

'That's right; it was used for rum smuggling.' He raised his eyebrows and then settled his eyes on her lips and leaned a little closer. 'Can I stop you there, and show you how much I love you?'

He kissed her, winding his fingers through her braided hair, then with one swift move pulled her on to his lap.

Serena lost all track of time and after more lovemaking Broderick poured champagne.

Once again, collapsing onto Serena's double bed, they explored each other's bodies. Later they cuddled and drifted into a deep, contented sleep.

It was the early hours of the morning when Serena lifted her head from the pillow. She felt a warm glow and a delicious tingle creep over her. She and Broderick had made love! And it was the best thing ever. She rolled over to grab him for some more loving, then felt only the pillow. He must have gone to his own room during the night. Ever the gentleman — though people would know.

Something cold caught on her fingers from his pillow — a string of beads. Lots of tiny, threaded, creamy shells.

Serena shivered when she saw the note. Something wasn't right. Her mouth went dry as parchment when she read the scribbled message.

Remember me always — Broderick xx

'Seriously? He thinks it's the thing, to flit into my life, have fun then disappear? What's wrong with that man?' Serena spoke to her reflection in the mirror while she used a cotton wool pad and apricot toner to wipe her face.

She'd got rather warm during the night and her cheeks were glowing with a radiance she'd never seen there before.

'Typical of my luck.' She sighed. 'He tells me the sad story and then does a bunk.'

Placing the necklace on the dressing table, she climbed back into bed. She was fully confident that he loved her — definitely he did — but why not stay? She sobbed herself back to sleep.

★ ★ ★

Morning sun flooded the room causing Serena to sit up. Then she remembered, wept a little and dried her tears. Sulking about things wasn't her style, and she was hungry for a bacon sandwich.

She fastened the necklace of shells around her neck and immediately she felt he was still there.

She was still in time for breakfast. She pulled on cut-off jeans and checked shirt, then made her way down to breakfast.

Broderick was on her mind. He'd told her about his daughter, little Aileen, and how he loved her. More than once he'd said those words to her, that was why he'd turned up, and proved it from the way he'd kissed her and made love so passionately. But why run away? It seemed to be a habit of his; yet wouldn't he want more of what they'd shared last night? She certainly did.

'Is your friend joining you for breakfast?' The landlady had a twinkle in her eye and it was obvious she'd been observant enough to realise they'd shared the evening together.

'No, he was called away.' She asked for a bacon sandwich and was really glad that the hotel catered for holiday-makers and the whims of Brits abroad. Over breakfast tea and a doorstopper butty (made as a special request) she couldn't get Broderick out of her mind, and how he loved her with such passion, as she loved him.

They hadn't discussed the future;

whether he would like her to meet Aileen, or if they would keep in touch. *He knows how much I love him, I told him enough times . . . Hang on; I didn't put it into words.* Serena put down her cup and concentrated. *Does it matter?* She frowned. *I definitely showed him, but actually, I didn't say it.*

Everything Serena tried to do came back to one thing — she needed to tell Broderick she loved him. Reading the note over and over, knowing him as she did, it became clear to her that he was afraid of getting close to the ones he loved. He'd swallowed his pride — made an effort to find her, especially after the way they'd parted.

The dark, handsome man had travelled across the sea, treated her to the best champagne and lobster — yet none of those things mattered. Being in his arms, feeling him breathing next to her just knowing he was there, that was enough.

It was time for him to stop dashing

off. And she needed to say loud and clear, 'I love you, Broderick Loveday.'

A huge Christmas tree was being bundled into the foyer as a couple of the hotel workers delved into a box of tinsel and baubles. The landlady was supervising and carols were playing on the radio. Serena had almost forgotten it was nearly Christmas. At home, her dad would be buying the biggest tree he could find in the market and her mum would be rustling up mince pies and sausage rolls for the carol singers and anyone who paid a visit.

She decided now would be a good time to ring home, and let them know she was all right.

'Yes, Mum, it's going well. I miss you, of course, and it won't be long before I'm on the plane and back home.'

She spoke to her dad, after apologising for waking them so early in the morning, and felt a lump in her throat hearing their voices, knowing she wouldn't be with them for Christmas.

'I'll be back before you know it, then we can celebrate New Year together.' She said her goodbyes, and wiped away a tear.

'Can I get you anything else?' The jolly hotel owner bustled around looking after everyone.

Serena shook her head. 'No, that was all excellent, thank you. Reminded me of home so much I had to ring my folks.' She smiled.

'As long as you're fuelled up for the day?'

'Absolutely, most definitely.' Serena patted her middle. 'Now I have a ferry to catch.'

★ ★ ★

Up in her room Serena grabbed a light jacket. She'd noticed a few clouds gathering, and a breeze was rustling the palm trees. A touch of lip gloss was all the make-up she needed; the outdoor life had given her a natural glow.

As she left the hotel, one of the

workers atop the ladder fixing a golden star on the tree shouted after her. 'Don't go too far, there's a change in the weather, and not for the better.'

Serena didn't mind about trivial things like weather. Hadn't she slept in a hammock, scrambled down a mountain and swum in a lake with the man she'd been in love with since she'd met him? Only she'd taken a while to realise it. His gentle manner and love of all things beautiful gave her an inner calm and he excited her more now she knew how it felt to lie naked beside him. His lovemaking was pure dynamite.

The Ruby Queen of the Caribbean was open for tourists, but Serena was looking for a small ferry — preferably leaving in the next half hour. A row of boats had *CLOSED* written across them and a rope barring anyone from boarding. Irritated, Serena hurried along — then in the distance, eating hot dogs, she spied Shami and Rhawand.

'Yes! Just the chaps I want.' Quickly

she sprinted along and caught up with her old friends.

'I need a ferry to the Island of Shells.' She didn't see the look of horror on their faces. 'There aren't many boats sailing today, from the looks of things.' She turned and scanned the empty vessels.

'You not heard the news, nor looked up there?' Shami raised his eyes skyward. 'There's a storm on the way, it's not safe to take the boats out. Even the fishermen are leaving it.'

'But you don't understand, I haven't got lots of days left here! If we go now, we should miss the storm and be back before it's begun.'

She wasn't prepared to stay on Kiri-Kiri and not see Broderick one last time.

'You eccentric English are crazy, and so must we be to even think about it.' Rhawand shook his head and looked at his mate. 'Then again, it's triple rates on storm days.'

'Will you close your trap?' Shami

slapped his friend's leg. 'On the boat, and quick, we'll get arrested again if anyone in authority sees us.' He whistled to the right and left. A couple of local looking guys appeared and ran with the two lads to the familiar craft tied up near the edge of the harbour wall.

'Jump in, and hold on tight.' Frowning as he revved the engine, Shami helped Serena aboard, and checked his mate and the new recruits were seated before he made a sweeping turn and headed out to sea. He looked back to check no one was watching. The boat swayed this way and that like a tin bath in the ocean.

Serena prayed . . . *Please let the forecast be wrong. It's so selfish of me, putting these lads to so much trouble.*

For once the forecast wasn't wrong — the storm blew in rapidly. Anything that wasn't tied down was blowing away on Kiri-Kiri — the streets were deserted. On the ocean, a small boat with four men and one woman quickly lost control as the cloudy sky turned to a black, angry tempest.

Serena, soaked to the skin, clung tightly to the rail at the edge of the boat. She was too frightened to speak. This was all her fault. At least the boys had made sure she'd worn a life jacket, and they were each wearing one too. Little consolation when she saw Shami being thrown across the other side of the boat and Rhawand take the wheel, struggling to keep control.

Her braids stuck to her head like rats' tails and her clothing made her cold and sticky. In a blink, she spotted one of the new recruits tumble overboard and she scrambled along the wooden benches to try and grab his arm. Even with a life jacket, a human being would be tossed around like a bobbin. She screamed and hung over the edge. 'Grab my hand; I'll pull you back on board.' She leaned further into the crashing waves and fished around for his hand.

Rhawand dragged Serena back onto

the boat. 'You can't try that! There's sharks down there, remember.' He hung over the edge, and in a couple of minutes, hauled his mate back onto the boat. 'That's how you do it. Now sit tight and we'll be over there in next to no time.'

Her heart beat so fast she wondered if she might have a heart attack before they could make it to the island. Now she wished she'd listened to people who knew far better than she did how bad the storms could be in the tropics. This was more of a hurricane than a storm, and far worse than anything she'd ever seen in her life. She hardly dare ask, and her voice sounded feeble when she spoke to Shami. 'Are we nearly there yet?'

Before he could answer, the whole boat hit a monster wave that thrust the boat and its occupants into a loop-the-loop of a gigantic surf ride, ending when Serena plunged deep into the water. A mouthful of brine filled her with a sense of sickness and fear.

Struggling to push herself upward and then gasp for breath when she finally surfaced took all her strength. Around her, shards of the boat swirled and floated. The pain in her chest from fear of never seeing her loved ones again overwhelmed her. More than that, for the safety of the lads — she tried to swim against the storm and hoped they were somewhere near, but couldn't see for the lashing rain and wind.

Unsure how long she'd been treading water, getting weaker as each moment passed, Serena couldn't keep awake any more. She'd shouted for the others, but it was using too much breath, and they were nowhere to be seen. The cold was taking hold of her bones and her teeth chattered, making her feel sick. She slid under the sea, sinking, not able to breathe . . .

Strong arms scooped her up and dragged her to the surface. Through the black and cold of the storm, Serena felt herself being dragged along until she was on firm ground. Someone was thumping her chest. A feeling of ghastly sickness washed over her, she was pushed onto her side and hard wooden flooring pressed against her mouth. She vomited and coughed and then the taste of seawater made her sick again. Her heart ached from the pummelling. Then she spluttered and took a gasp of breath, then tried to sit up.

'Serena, you're alive?'

She felt the warmth of his protective arms as they wound around her again. No mistaking who had pulled her from the sea. Now she could let him know.

'Broderick . . . ' her voice warbled from the brine. 'I love you.'

He wrapped a blanket around her and held her tight, stroking her hair.

'I know, and you didn't have to risk your life to tell me. I was thinking, we could get together permanently. I'll leave my reclusive life behind. There's a mansion in Buckinghamshire with a Serena-sized space in it — if you'll have me.'

Serena melted into his warmth and

knew she'd found the place she wanted to stay forever.

'Oh, I will,' she sighed.

Other titles in the
Linford Romance Library:

THE CHRISTMAS VISITOR

Jill Barry

Rich man's daughter Eleanor is horrified when her father invites disgraced nobleman Rupert to join the family Christmas house party. But when the pair meet by accident, she finds him attractive, then is dismayed to learn his identity. Rupert and his valet fit in well, while gentle scheming by the indispensable Mr Steadman enhances Eleanor and Rupert's dawning relationship. Upstairs and downstairs, romance blossoms — but can both his lordship and his valet make amends for their past mistakes?